Cindy Foley

THE RENEWAL

an *I, Clawed* adventure

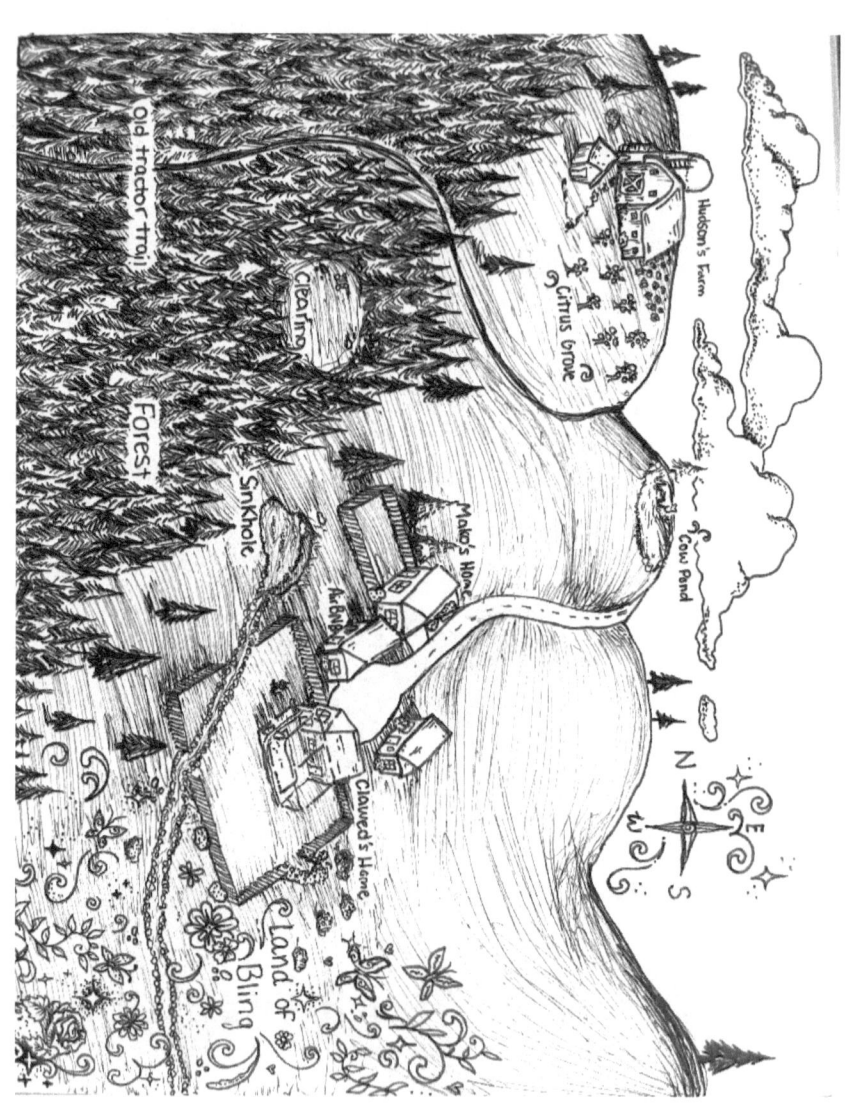

The Renewal - Book One of *I, Clawed's* adventures is a work of fiction. The cats Clawed and Gidget are real, but the other names, characters, places and incidents are the product of the author's imagination.

Any resemblance they may have to actual pets, people, or events is purely coincidental.

Many thanks to my brother Andrew Alix for reading and editing this book, but mostly for encouraging me to finish it.

A special thanks to my husband Dave for always asking me that one question that makes me scratch my head and sends me back to my desk.

Cover art: Arthur Doweko

Map: Krystal Reither

Microsoft Word Clip Art

Second Edition – 2023

ISBN: 9781734484670

CAST OF CHARACTERS

Clawed – author of these adventures

Tabbert – Clawed's friend, a Florida green anole

Tikky – an orange tabby, born in a barn, lives in the woods

Gidget – a tabby cat who comes to live with Clawed

Sage and Ben Foley – the humans that Clawed lives with

Dr. Furby – Clawed's veterinarian

Farmer Hudson – owns the barn, Meg is his daughter

Butch – Farmer Hudson's chocolate Labrador retriever

Max – Farmer Hudson's brother

Leroy – Max's dog

Nel – white horse in the barn

Orange – orange male cat that lives in the barn

Owie – gray tabby that was injured and came to live in the barn

Blinglings – magical creatures that live in Bling

       Stocker – main leader of Bling

       Lil – present Secretarycat

       Shep – a sheep, Lil's wise confidant

       Joey and Stevie – mice

       Piggy Pomp – a pig

       Necky – a giraffe

Lay-Z – a camel

Dilitz Maids – aquatic creatures that live in the butterfly pond

Romeo and Juliet – frogs

Tik, Tak, and Tuk – penguins

Curly and Larry - turtles

This story is dedicated to adored pets of all kinds and species

all over the world…

and to the people who love them.

Chapter 1

In the supernatural world

things aren't always what they seem.

When my friend Tabbert first told me there was a magical town called Bling on the other side of the rose arbor, I didn't believe him. If I hadn't eventually seen it for myself, I would tell you it was all pure hogwash (no offense to Piggy Pomp).

My name is Clawed, and I'm a writer. I'd better start at the beginning.

"A kitten is in the animal world

what a rosebud is in the garden." Robert Southey

Chapter 2

His humom

named him Clawed, as in…*not* declawed.

He was about six weeks old the day he was taken from his birth mother. It's not like he ever wanted to leave home.

To him, happily-ever-after meant living with Mother, his two brothers and four sisters, and a couple of dogs; oh, and a tarantula named Fuzzy Stanley. Umm…er…Clawed was still trying to figure out how he felt about spiders.

On that day, he was dreaming that he was floating on his

back in a stream. Wait. What?

"Yikes!" Clawed struggled to catch hold of something but his claws sliced through nothing. "Marnie, put me down!" The family's golden retriever picked Clawed up in her teeth. She gently placed him on the living room rug. Clawed was preparing to bolt away when she plopped down and grasped him between her front paws.

"You'd better stay right here, Squirt," she said. "Otherwise, Brutus might get you." Then lick, lick, slobber, slobber, slobber. Yuk!

Clawed accepted the licking. Marnie was his rock. Brutus the German Shepherd would have eaten him if not for Mother and Marnie. More than once, they'd sent him yelping to the back yard with a bloody nose.

As if six kittens, Mother, and the dogs weren't enough of a menagerie, two adults and their three kids lived at our house, too. Catching a quiet catnap was impossible.

Still, this was home.

The afternoon heat and Marnie's licking made him sleepy again, and the usual chaos seemed to be at an all-time low.

"Yawwnnn...."

Honk. Honk!

Kids ran through the house. "Somebody's here."

Marnie leapt up. Knocking Clawed aside with her tree-trunk leg, she ran to the breezeway.

Clawed tumbled whisker over tea kettle. The screams and Marnie's barking hurt his ears. His fur stood on end, like he'd gotten his tail stuck in a light socket.

Heart pounding, he ran under the couch. The TV was on, but for some reason the strangers outside held his interest.

Clawed loved watching TV. He also liked to read, partially because he was so curious, but mostly because he also liked to write, and writers needed to know stuff. He needed to know what was going on.

He snuck around the perimeter of the living room, slipped behind the curtains, and peeked out the sliding glass door that opened onto the breezeway.

The Mom stood in the driveway talking to a strange lady who looked like a forest fairy Clawed had seen on the Disney channel. A breeze blew her long hair around her shoulders. It shined in the sun like a cape made of spider webs.

He couldn't hear what The Mom and the lady were saying. After a few minutes, they came into the breezeway. Clawed stayed behind the curtain. It was usually a good hiding spot.

Not that day.

After scooping up his brothers and sisters one by one, then putting them down, The Mom spotted him and handed me into the stranger's arms. "This is Clawed."

He didn't struggle. New things were interesting. He sniffed. "Mmm. Purrfect." She smelled good, not like dog or kid sweat. Clawed ducked his head into her arm pit and wiggled closer. He wasn't even scared. Well, maybe a little. There was comfort in those smell-good arms.

Mother meowed in the background. "Clawed! Be still! Don't scratch."

Clawed figured he'd better do what she said. Mother could give a nasty swat when we misbehaved.

"Good boy, Clawed," Mother whispered. "This could be it!"

"It? What does that mean?" Clawed asked.

The smell-good lady put him down and picked up his brother, Meatball. He was Clawed's opposite, all white.

Clawed scooted back to the living room.

"Get out there." Mother hissed and boxed his ears.

"Why?"

"Stop asking questions. It's time for you to go make your own way."

5

"Why?" Where was he going and what did she mean, "…make your own way?"

Mother hissed and swatted him again.

Clawed ran out to the breezeway. Legs towered over him, The Mom was saying 'pleased to meetcha,' a man with the lady was saying 'oh what a cute kitty.' They picked kittens up and put them down. Lunch crunchies tumbled in Clawed's belly. Meatball barfed on the rug.

Marnie had stopped barking, but her heavy, wagging tail was as dangerous as little Mikey swinging a baseball bat. Something was bound to go flying.

Call it sixth sense or whatever, but *something* different was coming of all this.

Lady Smellgood picked Clawed up again. "Aren't you funny looking with those bald spots above your eyes?" Bald spots? Had Marnie licked half the fur off his face?

The lady turned to the man standing beside her. "What do you think, Ben?"

"I like black," he said.

Lady Smellgood didn't put Clawed back down, but held him closer.

He melted into her warmth.

"We'll take this one," she said.

6

Who…me? Take me where?

She walked away from the crowd, and the chaos of Clawed's life began to fade.

Mother mewled. "I love you, Clawed. Don't worry, you'll be fine."

He'd never heard Mother mewl before. He poked his head out from under the lady's arm. "It's okay, Mother."

He swallowed a strange lump in his throat. "I'm going to make my own way," whatever that meant. "See you later!"

He didn't see Mother later…or ever again.

 It had been a year since Clawed moved here. This was the way it was always supposed to be. He knew that now.

Actually, he knew a lot of things. He understood human talk and learned things by reading the computer over Sage's (Lady Smellgood) shoulder and watching TV with Ben. *Jeopardy* was one of his favorite shows.

As he grew in this new, peaceful household, he came to realize, there was more to life than meets the cat's eye.

Like he'd mentioned earlier; his new friend Tabbert told him that out beyond the rose arbor was the magical Town of Bling where the Blinglings live.

Clawed couldn't see them.

It's one thing to be curious and learn things. It's another to figure out if what you learn is credible—or not.

Tabbert was his friend, did that mean he had to believe him?

So—was magic real? Clawed had to get out to the garden to figure that out. But under his current circumstances, that was going to be difficult.

He wasn't allowed to go out.

Chapter 3

Tabbert

a Florida green anole with rotating eyes could be quite annoying. Clawed learned a lot about him after watching a documentary about lizards on Animal Planet.

His feet differed from most lizards in that each toe had adhesive pads that enabled him to cling to vertical surfaces such as windows, stucco walls, fence posts, and aluminum gutters.

Tabbert clung to the gutter downspout outside the screened-in pool patio. Clawed was sitting on his cat tower situated on the back patio inside the screen.

"Hey, Clawed," he said. "Nice collar. I like red."

Clawed rolled his eyes. Wearing a neck choker wasn't his favorite thing in the world, but he was pleased by Tabbert's flattery. Or—was he up to something?

"You're cool. I've seen you when Tikky comes around."

Clawed bit back a snarl.

Not seeming to notice Clawed's sudden discomfort, Tabbert babbled on. "You sit in there watching him...like 'whatever'." Tabbert shrugged his right shoulder and snorted. Then he spun around and looked directly into Clawed's eyes. "I looked like you just then, right? Hey, what's a lizard's favorite side dish? French flies." He laughed at his own joke.

Clawed resisted the urge to roll his eyes again.

"Meowww!"

"There she goes again" Tabbert scooted a few feet away, captured a bug. He scooted back. "I wonder why she does that," he mumbled in between swallowing. "Mm mm...good."

"Gidget's been weird ever since she came here. I still haven't figured out why she carries around that stuffed mouse. Anyway, I'm not partial to bugs," Clawed said, "but they are fun to play with."

"There aren't any bugs in Bling. Tikky ought to hang out in there more often. Maybe his fleas would go away."

Clawed coughed, as if a hairball had gotten stuck in his throat. "Bling? Blingedy, blingedy, bling, bling, bling. Is that all you think about? What kind of a name is that anyway?" He gulped, licked his paw and swiped it over the back of his ear.

"I don't know," Tabbert answered. "What is a name anyway? Just a word somebody made up, a bunch of letters put together by someone who attached a capital letter and assigned meaning, an inspiration erupting…"

"Okay, okay!" Clawed raised a paw to stop Tabbert's philosophical tirade which was almost impossible once Tabbert really got going. "Bling's a nice name," he said. "But I never heard of it before, not as a place anyway."

"What do you mean, 'not as a place'?"

"By definition, the word 'bling' means something flashy or elaborately glittery, like Sage's blouse, the one covered with round mirror thingies (did he really say 'thingies') that blind me when the sun shines on them. 'Bling' doesn't mean a place."

Clawed could be a major player on *Jeopardy*.

"But I've never heard of the *town* of Bling, or Blinglings for that matter," he said.

"It's right over there." Tabbert gestured toward the garden on the hill behind the screen enclosure.

"What is?"

"Bling; duh, that is what we were talking about."

"Bling is the butterfly garden?"

Tabbert snorted. "It's a town. You know…where Blinglings live, hellOo!"

Clawed pressed his nose against the screen and squinted. "I see flowers and bees. Sometimes I see you running around out there; but I sure don't see a town. You know I see Sage when she's weeding or Ben mowing the yard. Once in a while, Meg goes by on her way to the woods, and the boys are skateboarding on their ramp on top of the hill.

"Sometimes I see armadillos or possums. One time, a possum fell out of the pine tree. Oh, and turtles. Do you know turtles come by almost every day?"

"Yes, yes, I know." Tabbert did pushups on the screen. "Turtles come by every day, and I know about the raccoons, and I know about the cats that bug you, and the bugs that bug you. By the way, I also know that you catch the brown lizards that get inside your screen. I wish you wouldn't eat them. You never know. You don't want to get confused and eat one of my family."

Hmm.

Tabbert continued. "But honestly, Clawed, don't you see me disappear out here sometimes?" He laughed. "See me disappear? Get it? How can you see me if I disappear? That's funny."

12

"Tabbert, I thought that was because you're a lizard. You know, changing color and all that."

"That too." Tabbert posed like a model. He placed one toe on his cheek and flicked his tail back and forth. "Pretty cool, huh?"

"You're so vain."

"Anyway!" Tabbert went on. "As soon as I pass through the rose arbor, I'm there. Haven't you ever seen me...or I mean, not seen me, even though you thought I was right there?"

Clawed frowned, his forehead furrowing with doubt. Tabbert remained quiet, a difficult task for him.

"I don't know. I never really thought about it."

"What's to think about? Either you saw me or you didn't." Tabbert's tail switched back and forth again. His dewlap flared; a sure sign he was getting frustrated.

Clawed yawned and stretched. "I think I'll go inside and see what's on TV. Nice talking to you."

"Please." Tabbert stared through the screen. "Let me finish. I'm your friend, right? Don't go getting all huffy. Listen! I need to tell you about Bling. Please!"

Clawed sat down again.

Tabbert continued. "I've always known two worlds, Bling

13

and 'here' where you live with your peeps."

It probably wasn't easy explaining something he'd always known, something that even Clawed couldn't understand. Try explaining the taste of a June bug to someone who's never eaten one.

Tabbert said he thought everybody knew about Bling. But perhaps he was beginning to find out—not everybody did.

"Okay," Tabbert continued. "When you were still allowed out, you know, before you stepped on the nail, er...I mean—got in a fight with Tikky, I don't suppose you saw anything when you came by the garden?"

"Like, what would I see?" Clawed growled, couldn't help it.

"You okay, Clawed?"

"I'm hungry, that's all. Can you get on with it so I can go in and have lunch?"

"Okay, okay. There's the mice brothers, Joey and Stevie. They don't look like they have any legs or feet, but they do, and they sort of glide when they walk. All the Blinglings do. Strange, right? They have black eyes and see-through-ish bodies with a bunch of angles that glitter, kind of like diamonds. You can see rainbows on their skin when the light hits them."

14

"See-through-ish? Hmmm. So, inside Bling, you turn different colors?"

"I don't know. I haven't looked at myself in there."

Clawed looked at Tabbert over the bridge of his nose. "You do know that according to the Discovery Channel, the American chameleon, also known as Anolis carolinensis, is renowned for its ability to change color. When you're on a green leaf, you're green. On tree bark, you turn brown. God made chameleons so they could hide no matter where they went."

"Renowned, huh!" Tabbert sat up straighter. "Of course, I know that. Wait!" With a flick of his tail, Tabbert spun in a circle, his 'I've got a revelation' maneuver. "That's it! That must be why my family became messengers, because we can blend in with all our surroundings so well."

He barely took a breath as he chattered on. "And then, there's Piggy Pomp, and Necky, and on yeah…Lil. She helps Stocker run the place."

"Who's Stocker?"

"I've never met him, but they tell me he's the leader, like the President."

"Uh, huh." Doubtful, Clawed blinked and shook his head.

"Clawed, you have to believe me on this one for now.

15

Bling *is* a real place. My friends Piggy Pomp, Joey and Stevie, and Lil, they all live there. Lil is a cat just like you...sort of."

"What do you mean—sort of? Either she's a cat or she's not. What do Blinglings do, anyway? And I'm not saying I believe you yet. I just want to know. Why are they there? And, if they *are* there, why can't I see them?"

"Gosh, Clawed," Tabbert said. "I don't know why you can't see them. I mean, when you were allowed out, did you ever walk through the garden?"

"Of course, I did. A lot of those brown lizards live there. And butterflies..."

"Oh my gosh, you know them?"

"No...," I answered. "Why would I want to know a butterfly anyway?" They were fun to watch, flitting about as they do. Once, he tried to catch one. Just when he'd figured out which way it was going, it swerved. Clawed had flipped and swiped mid-air but didn't catch it. "A mouthful of butterfly isn't all that interesting anyway," he said. "The wings leave a weird dryness on my tongue, like I've just eaten a cotton ball."

"Honestly, Clawed. Anyway, Bling has always been there, at least as long as I can remember."

"How long can that be," Clawed muttered. Green anoles

definitely don't live as long as cats do. He'd learned that on *Jeopardy* too. That alarmed him for a second. He didn't want to think about losing him as a friend.

"Smarty," Tabbert raised his nose and turned away. You think you know everything? Okay how about this one? What do you call a prehistoric lizard that's exercised too much? Dino-sore. Get it?" He almost fell off the screen he was laughing so hard. "Oh, by the way, next week is the Blingling Fair, *and* it's my birthday."

"I thought last month was your birthday."

"Right!"

Tabbert celebrated his birthday every month. Why not? Clawed smiled. "Cool. Let's have a party."

"Are you even listening?" Tabbert spun like a dog chasing its tail. Even though the screen separated them, he was only inches from Clawed's face. Used to his whirling dervish act, Clawed didn't even flinch.

"I know!" Tabbert's eyes glittered with excitement. "Lil can explain it better than me. She's the one who told me to tell you about them. Something's wrong. Bling needs help. There must be a way I can help you understand! Wait here. I've got to talk to Lil."

He ran down the gutter spout, stopped when he reached

17

the ground, and looked back at Clawed. Then, he gestured with one sticky toe toward Sage's garden, "Look. It's sick."

Yes, he could see the garden. And now that Tabbert mentioned it, even with Sage's daily care, it didn't look the same as it had. Blossoms were droopy. Leaves were curling and brown at the edges.

Tabbert turned and scooted away. "I'll be back."

He ran through the rose arbor at the entrance to the garden. Then, just like Tabbert said he would, he disappeared right before Clawed's eyes.

"Hmph."

Clawed had been out in that garden plenty of times. How could Tabbert expect him to believe something he'd never seen or even touched?

It all seemed a bit farfetched, but then you're probably thinking—so is a cat who talks to lizards.

Once, while listening to Sage's iPhone app, "Enjoying Everyday Life," Clawed learned that sometimes you've got to take some things on faith because, somewhere deep in your gut, you know they're right. Tabbert had never given Clawed a reason to doubt him before, so he decided then and there to trust him.

Besides, who in the world could make up a story like that if it weren't true? Time for a nap. Things had a way of sorting themselves out with a good nap.

Right about then, Tikky sauntered past the back fence. Remembering their…er…confrontation, Clawed settled his head between his paws and closed his eyes to very thin slits. Hopefully, it would look like he was asleep.

Chapter 4

Clawed's not-so-good friend Tikky

was a scruffy, orange mess. His fur was matted and dirty. He rarely washed.

He hung around Sage and Clawed's yard and strutted by the back fence at least twice a day pretending like he didn't see Clawed sitting up on his cat tower inside the screened-in porch.

Clawed was sure Tikky could see him. He could tell by the way he flicked his tail as he went by.

Tikky often sprayed his scent on Sage's prized rose arbor or on the St. Francis Patron Saint of Nature statue. So rude.

One afternoon when Clawed was still allowed to go outside (It was all Tikky's fault that he couldn't. Clawed still growled under his breath every time he thought about it.) he found Tikky sprawled out under a bush in the front yard.

Clawed snarled. His claws twitched. "Hey. What are you doing here?"

"Yawwnnn." Tikky squinted into the sun, stood, stretched, then lay back down. "Go away."

Forcing a congenial smile, Clawed sat back, then washed his face and smoothed his fur. "Excuse me?"

"This is my yard." His mouth stretched open with another yawn. He sat up. "You get the back yard. I get the front. Kapeesh? Comprende'? Now, scram."

Clawed's hackles rose. He thrust my face into Tikky's. "*I* live here. *You* do not."

Maybe this big bully wasn't used to back talk from any critter. He stood and tried to stare Clawed down. "Since when?"

Big cat, yessiree!

Not.

Tikky had a lot more fluff than substance, so he looked bigger than he really was. At the moment, Clawed didn't know that, and wasn't about to show that Tikky's size intimidated him.

Well—one comment led to another and next thing you

21

know, Tikky took a swipe at Clawed, his dirty claws barely missing Clawed's face. In a cat's breath, Clawed pinned Tikky to the ground by the neck. He resorted to a pitiful tactic and yowled. "Uncle!"

The minute Clawed let him go, Tikky turned tail and ran.

Clawed chased him to the edge of a vast evergreen forest that separated his house from the Hudson's farm.

"This is my yard." Clawed hissed, "And, don't forget it." He returned back to his own yard. A stabbing pain jabbed him in the bottom of his right, front foot. He limped the rest of the way. When he reached the stoop, he lay down and licked his wound. It was bleeding. Good thing he was left-pawed.

Three days later, he could barely walk on it.

"That doesn't look good. Come on Clawed." Sage picked him up. "We'll have the vet take a look at that."

If she didn't have such a strong clamp around him, he'd have run. Being a bit claustrophobic, Clawed hated being stuffed into the carrier. "I'll be good," he meowed. "Let me ride on the seat, please!"

"Get in there. It's safer for you." Sage gave him a firm push and quickly locked the door.

"Grrr…" Clawed was not having a good day.

The waiting room at the vet's office was an ear-splitting nightmare. Leashed dogs barked at hissing cats. Momentarily glad that he was confined to his portable carrier, Clawed huddled within its dark safety until Dr. Beverly Furby reached in and gently lifted him out. Her curly hair reminded him of a poodle.

"Hello, Clawed." She cuddled him and scratched behind his ears before setting him onto the examining table. "Hurt yourself, did you?" She glanced at Sage. "What happened?"

"I'm not sure. I heard a strange yowl a few days ago when I was out working in the garden. A few minutes later, I found Clawed sitting by the front door. I didn't think much more about it until yesterday when I saw him limping and found blood on the tile floor."

Poodle-hair shown a light into his eyes. "What happened, Clawed?"

He didn't say anything and wasn't about to admit that he'd gotten hurt stepping on a rusty roofing nail, even if he had been chasing a bully away. Where was the glory in that?

Dr. Furby clamped Clawed under her arm, then examined the bottom of his foot. She had a strong grip. He couldn't wrench his paw free. "Looks like a puncture wound? Is he an outside cat?"

"Yes…sometimes. But not at night."

Uh oh. Clawed waited for what was coming next, another lecture about the perils of allowing cats to play outside.

"Mm, hm." The vet cleaned and bandaged the wound. Then, out came the needle.

"Ouch." Clawed tried not to cry, but couldn't help himself. Was there anyone who liked shots?

"I know. You're a good boy, Clawed." Dr. Furby cuddled him once more before putting him back in the carrier. He didn't eat the treat she offered (until later).

She handed Sage a small, orange bottle. "Here's an antibiotic. Two times a day by mouth, preferably with a meal. It would be better if Clawed stays inside from now on."

Clawed meowed. "Ain't happening."

Boy, was he ever wrong.

Back at home, Clawed sat by himself on the couch. He was angry: at Tikky for trying to bully him, at his stupid foot for getting infected even though he'd been washing it several times a day, and at Sage for taking him to the vet.

"I hate that he has to stay inside," Sage said. "I want him to be able to experience his true cat self."

Okay, maybe he'd forgive Sage.

24

"I don't want him getting hurt again," Ben said.

Okay, so now Clawed was mad at him.

"Neither do I, but…"

Ben picked up the newspaper. "I still miss Lil. I don't want to lose him now."

Lil? The same cat that Tabbert said is the secretary-cat of Bling? She'd lived here before he did? Clawed felt betrayed. He decided to be mad at everybody, including Tabbert who was trying to get him to believe that there was something magical out there, something beyond the black and white of what he saw every day. Hog wash.

Clawed limped out to the porch, climbed to the top of his tower, and chewed on his bandage.

A spot of sun warmed his carpet. Nap time. It had been a long day indeed. He closed his eyes. "Ahh."

Next day, he wasn't allowed out, and then the next. Were they seriously going to make him stay in?

Clawed cried as loud as he could when Sage talked about letting me go back out. Ben stuck to his guns. Clawed's foot already felt better. For days, he clawed the furniture, pulled threads out of the upholstery, and gouged the door jambs next to the door handles.

Ben yelled at him. "Clawed, stop."

"You're not going out," Sage said.

Traitors.

That didn't stop Clawed from trying. He did his best to wear them down. He even tried biting Ben once and received a slap on the nose for it. He felt bad about that and angry at the same time.

In the meantime, he resorted to pretending not to see the mangy ball of dirty fluff swaggering by outside.

"I don't care," Clawed muttered under his breath as he licked his injured paw.

Tikky probably had a bad case of fleas and, probably, ear mites too. See him scratching, trying to get that itch...right there...that's it...between his shoulder blades. He couldn't reach it. Ha, ha! The fool fell over backward. Served him right.

Clawed had to figure a way to get outside so that he could investigate Bling, but more importantly, he didn't want Tikky getting too comfortable hanging around his yard.

Chapter 5

A cat has nine lives

for three it plays, for three it stays, and for the last three it stays.

Gidget's first life began under Max's house trailer where she was born.

A hungry cat, her striped fur matted and dull, snuck out of the woods and climbed through a small hole in the skirting at the back of the trailer. It was almost time. The kittens were coming.

Something about the darkness of the underbelly of the trailer attracted the mother cat. Maybe it was the closeness to one of Leroy's food plates that had drawn the pregnant cat. Several were scattered about the yard.

Maybe Fate had sent the cat there. Who could understand

Fate's reasons for doing anything?

Maybe it was the warmth of the dusty bed sheet she'd found a week ago, blown under there by a careless summer wind after Leroy had pulled it off the line.

The mother cat tugged and pawed at it until she'd pulled it to the darkest recess she could find. Tamping and kneading, she turned around and around pulling at the outer edges of the sheet until she'd made a bowl-like birthing den.

As the contractions overtook her, she silently gave in to the process. Not a groan or a whimper escaped as her body tensed and relaxed several times until she gave birth to two tiny kittens. That was all. The mother was skinny from lack of food. Her slight milk supply might barely feed them.

When the birthing process was done, and she'd licked the babies clean, she pulled them close. The gray and brown tabby kneaded and nuzzled at a barely swollen breast. The other kitten did not suckle. Although mother cat licked and licked the tiny body, the heart did not beat.

After she'd rested, mother cat pulled herself up. She tucked the bed sheet around the living kitten and gently picked up the other in her teeth. She carried it to the other end of the trailer, set it down in a hole she dug, and covered it with dirt. There were no tears as she left it, only a dull ache in her heart.

Without a sound, she tip-toed slowly to the hole in the trailer skirting, her nostrils flaring as she sniffed for food. Hyper alert, she stuck her head out, leery of the man who lived in the trailer with a huge, mean dog.

Max wore greasy, brown shirts and matching oil-stained pants. His dark green El Camino was spotless and ran like a top. He combed his hair by running dirty hands through it several times a day and whacked it a couple times a year with a pair of sewing scissors.

Clutter dominated the living room where he sat. The chair arms were black with sweat and grime. Broken down vehicles and car parts littered the yard.

Max had lived this way all his life; didn't see it as a mess. The house was comfortable. Everything in it was just "stuff" and didn't mean nothin' to him.

He hated cats with a passion. About the only thing besides cars that Max cared about was his dog.

Leroy slept on the bed, ate left-overs off Max's supper plate, and held a revered spot on the lumpy couch while Max watched TV. He drank out of a bucket that sat under an ever-dripping water spigot outside and ate out of pans strewn around the yard.

Most of the time Leroy wolfed down whatever Max put in his dish; but that morning as Leroy began to eat, a squirrel sitting on a branch overhead dropped a pine cone smack dab into Leroy's dish.

Startled, Leroy leapt back. While the chattering squirrel scurried from limb to limb, Leroy yelped and jumped around in a frenzy, shedding fur, scattering dog food, and kicking up dirt.

Mother cat watched from her dark shelter until Leroy settled down. He sniffed the ground, gobbling up dirty kibbles that he found here and there. After eating his fill, he drank from the water bucket, then lumbered out to the front yard to take a nap under a broken-down Chevy Max used for parts.

Mother cat waited and listened. Her stomach growled. Hearing the quiet mewling of her  newborn, she stepped through the hole. Crouching low and slinking close to the ground, she found one dirty morsel, then another, and another. Keeping a wary eye out for Leroy, she quickly stopped at his water pot before darting back under the trailer.

Over time, sometimes hungry, sometimes fed, the kitten grew in the dark warmth of the rumpled bed sheet. After a few weeks, her eyes opened. Not yet knowing what there was to see, she peered into the blackness, innately understanding that she had to stay where she was.

As she grew, she became more curious of her surroundings. Mother was often gone, so she pulled herself around in the bed bowl and explored the dirty folds of the sheet.

Some days Mother didn't return at all.

By the end of a month, the kitten could see gray shadows and then darkness, the dusty, charcoal outlines of objects and then darkness again. Not yet understanding the difference between night and day, she cried from hunger. Only when Mother came back and pulled her close did the baby eat and sleep comfortably.

The day the kitten found her way to the opening under the trailer, Mother had been gone a very long time. Hungry and mewing, the kitten had explored recesses and discarded objects under the trailer searching for her.

When she happened upon the hole in the skirting, she recognized Mother's scent on it. With her last bit of strength, she pulled herself up and out through the hole just as Leroy

31

came around the corner.

Momentarily blinded by the bright sun, she didn't see him barreling toward her. She screamed when he snatched her up in his teeth. "Mother!"

Whining, Leroy ran circles around the trailer with his mouth closed around the kitten. He dropped her on the ground, then shoved his nose into her face, then leaped back bounding and jumping around her. His huge feet landed so close to her,

 she was certain she'd be pounded to death. His barking made her ears ring.

Max yelled from inside. "Shut Up!"

Leroy kept barking.

Max poked his head out the door, then came out onto the porch. "Tarnation! Leroy's got himself a kitten." He laughed as Leroy picked up the kitten and tossed it in the air with a flip of his head, ran after it, picked it up from where it landed, and tossed it in the air again.

Through the scuffle, neither Max nor Leroy saw the Mother Cat dash out of the woods and across the yard. She leaped onto the dog's back. Two litters of kittens before this one had been lost to this junkyard dog. Mother Cat would fight for the life of her one remaining kitten, to the death this time if she had to.

Digging her claws through his fur into his skin, she bit down hard on the dog's neck.

Leroy howled.

Mother Cat clung to his neck with claws as sharp as knives. Leroy dropped to the ground and rolled. Mother Cat still held. Leroy leaped up, spun in a frenzy, ran, dropped and rolled again.

"Hey!" Max yelled and banged on the porch railing. He yelled again, louder. "HEY!" Max stomped back inside, yanked open the gun cabinet, and grabbed his rifle. "I'm going to get me some cat!"

He ran back to the door and had barely stepped onto the porch before firing off a shot. The wrestling cat and dog stopped for a brief second.

Mother Cat leaped off Leroy and ran like her tail was on fire. Another loud explosion sent metal bird-shot whizzing over her head. One nicked her ear. Miraculously, she stumbled over the kitten, grabbed it in her teeth, and ran. Leroy chased after her, so close she could almost feel his breath on her heels.

"Leroy!" max was still yelling from the porch. "Get out of the way, you stupid mutt!" Another shot barely missed as Mother Cat reached the woods and ducked under a log.

Leroy gave up at the edge of the woods, sniffed the log,

and remained there barking and whining.

With the kitten held securely in her teeth, Mother Cat scrambled out from under the log and kept running.

Deep in the woods, she stopped running and gasped for breath. She found a hole in the trunk of a rotting oak, slipped inside it, turned around several times, and lay down. Gently setting the kitten on the soft earthy loam between her front paws, she willed herself to breathe evenly and struggled to calm her pounding heart. Chirping to her kitten, she pulled it to her breast.

"Eat, little one. You have to be strong. That bully is only the first of many perils that will come along in your life." Curled into a ball around her baby, she forced herself to purr while licking her kitten down its back and across its face.

Then, she felt a slight movement. The kitten began to nurse.

"Yes," Mother Cat said. "You're a survivor."

Gidget didn't know about that. All she wanted to do was cuddle with Mother in the safe recesses of the bed sheet. It wasn't long before Mother let her know. That wasn't not happening.

Chapter 6

In the magic town of Bling

a multi-flora rose bush announced the comings and goings of anyone who passed through the lofty arch of its supporting arbor. The mystical plant hummed upon the arrival or departure of friends and family or vibrated with a grating, scratching alarm when strangers appeared.

The blooms hummed quietly. Shep, a wise Blingling sheep, peered between blades of strawberry grass he was pruning. A green anole dashed through the arbor and out of the garden. Tabbert in a hurry. No surprise there.

Cocking his head to one side, Shep sat back. The flowers' song didn't seem as strong as usual. Deciding that he must be imagining it, he shook his head and continued with his task.

Clawed was sitting on his tower when Tabbert returned. He clung upside down to the gutter downspout.

Clawed pawed the screen. "I'm glad you're back." His claw stuck. When he yanked it free, the screen ripped. Oops.

"Clawed, Stop!" Sage and Ben's authoritative tones reached him from inside. It wasn't their fault; they didn't know Tabbert was back. Clawed wanted to tell him that he'd seen him disappear. Sounded weird when he said it. By the way he was flicking his tail and zipping around, Clawed assumed he had something important to share.

"This isn't a joke, right?" Tabbert was still trying to convince him that Bling and its curious inhabitants were real.

"Right."

"So, you're saying, a rose bush announces?" Clawed asked.

"Definitely," he said. "A low, hum resonates from the base of the petals when I show up, or it rubs its branches together as a warning. The Blinglings can hear it, and only a few others—like me." Tabbert puffed out his chest with importance.

"Of course, you can," Clawed said doubtfully. Although he had decided to trust Tabbert, this was yet another incredible thing he was asking Clawed to swallow.

"Really, Clawed. Listen. Before you came, Sage and Ben had a calico named Lil. She lived nine lives with them and is on her tenth in Bling where she serves as Stocker's assistant."

So that explained the cat before. What was she doing out in the garden? How come he'd never seen her?

Tabbert babbled on. "Lil often gives me messages for the Blinglings. Once in a while the messages are for you. You know how sometimes I warn you of impending storms?"

Clawed nodded. Tabbert didn't need to warn him about storms. He watched the weather with Ben every day.

"I told you about the drought."

Clawed nodded again. "Uh huh." That had been in the news for months now. One artesian well spigot out in the yard had stopped flowing a week ago. He sat there thinking, 'tell me something I don't know.'

"But I didn't tell you about the treasure chest."

Clawed paid attention then. "What treasure chest?"

"First, let me tell you what happened when I went to find Lil."

Clawed looked outside through the screen. Would he ever get back outside so he could go see Bling for himself?

Having gone through the rose arbor, Tabbert scurried past the blueberry flax and onto the cobbled path that led to a crystal-clear pond. He stopped at the edge of the rock-lined basin that Ben had built for butterflies and squirrels. Groundwater from an artesian well sprayed into the air from a fountain in the middle.

Rainbows reflected off of drops of water clinging to leaves of a weeping hibiscus that dangled over the water. Or were the multi-colored droplets actually Blinglings busy at their work?

Something was off. Was the fountain smaller than usual? Tabbert looked into the pond. Shadows lurked in the shallows. He'd heard about the Dilitz maids that slipped amongst the depths, but he'd never seen them, wasn't sure he wanted to. Was the water level lower than usual?

He followed the path around the pond. On the other side, the path became a pebbled stream bed that ran alongside flower beds before disappearing into the ground. Strange, the stream bed was dry. Tabbert had never seen it dry.

How the water cycled was part of the magic of Bling. If

the water disappeared, what would happen to Bling? Tabbert couldn't talk to humans. That's why he needed Clawed's help, to convince Sage and Ben that the garden was in trouble.

Tabbert continued along the garden path. He stopped when he came upon a pigling napping under a periwinkle. "Piggy Pomp! Where's Lil?"

"Yawwnnn. Oink, snort, yawwnnn…yum." Piggy opened one eye a small slit, then closed it again.

"Piggy!" Tabbert called.

She lifted her head and blinked sleepy eyes into the sunlight. "Tabbert, can't you see I'm busy?"

He skittered over and nipped his plump little friend on the rump. "Wake up! I need to know where Lil is."

"Squeal! Oink…" Piggy frowned. "Why do you always come in here upsetting things and running around like you're demon possessed? Chillax, will you? What's so important that you have to disturb my sleep? I have to look my best at the fair next week. I've *got* to win a lottery ticket. Go away Tabbert! You're really quite bothersome!"

"Where's Lil?" Tabbert demanded again.

Piggy Pomp did not reply.

Frustrated, Tabbert scooted out from under the periwinkle. "Lil! ……. Lil!"

"MEOWWW." A heart-wrenching cry pierced the brilliant day, pitiful—as though something or someone were regurgitating a ball of misery from the bowels of their soul.

The micelings, Joey and Stevie, shivered in their burrow.

"Who's that caterwauling out there?" Joey asked.

"I don't know!" Shivering, Stevie huddled closer to his brother.

"I hear Tabbert out there. He's calling for Lil. I'll ask him. Maybe he knows." Joey scooted toward the burrow opening.

Stevie pulled him back by the tail. He whispered between clenched teeth. "Don't go out there."

Joey struggled to get free. "Let me go!"

Stevie was stronger. "You're not going out there! I'm scared! That sounds like …What if…" As Stevie attempted to explain, he let loose of his brother's tail. Joey slid away.

He stopped at the burrow opening and peered through the grass. He cautiously slipped onto the path just as Tabbert came running by.

"MMMEEEOOOWWWWW!!!" Very loud this time.

Startled, Joey leapt with fright and collided with Tabbert.

40

The mouse-chameleon ball rolled and scrabbled in the dirt; ears and noses filling with dust.

Tabbert's tongue flicked in and out. When his feet caught hold of solid ground, he dashed away. Joey slid back to his nest.

"I told you not to go out there," Stevie whispered angrily. "You're lucky you weren't eaten."

"Oh, be quiet!" Joey said. "You're a big chicken."

"No, I'm not. I know better than to go out during the day, especially when trouble's brewing."

"You don't even know what's going on," Joey whispered.

"All I know is it doesn't *sound* good, and that's enough for me." Stevie sat back on his haunches. "And look who's calling who a big chicken."

Joey muttered something under his breath as he rubbed his dusty whiskers on Stevie's side.

"What did you say?"

"I said..." Joey shook his head and sneezed, "... that it seems awfully dry out there."

Tabbert scooted under a rock to catch his breath. His heart thumped in his chest; his eyes were wide and glassy. He recognized the cry.

41

No one else in Bling knew Gidget, the brownish-gray tabby who lived with Clawed. She kept to herself. Tabbert had seen her, had even tried speaking with her, but she was a cat of few words.

Muttering to himself, Tabbert hurried on his way. "Got to talk to Lil."

He didn't find her…that day.

But Tabbert was a determined fellow, because he was still trying to explain Bling and its inhabitants to Clawed. As he talked on and on, Clawed wondered if he'd ever get to meet the cat named Lil or see this so-called magical town.

Chapter 7

The treasure chest

was protected by the Dilitz maids, or so Tabbert said.

"A singing rose bush and now a treasure chest." Clawed licked his paw and swiped it across the top of his head. "You said you were going to find Lil, that you were coming right back, and then you didn't."

"I know. She was busy with whatever she and Stocker do. I already told you. Stocker's the big muhah. Everybody knows that."

"And the Blinglings?" Clawed's whiskers drooped into a scowl. "I'm having a hard time wrapping my head around that one. They're shiny and faceted like very *good* cut glass, some with black eyes," he said. "And no legs."

"Well, they do have legs, but not like yours. Mostly, they slip along like snails, and their bodies reflect rainbows."

He had to be kidding. No way. Fairy tales.

Clawed immediately felt bad for thinking that. Sometimes you have to believe in your friend, or at least, let him think you do.

He tried to envision these strange creatures that looked like animals but slid like snails. There wasn't anything like that on *Jeopardy*. He couldn't imagine Tabbert with no legs, gliding along. Would he be able to run as fast as he usually did?

"Strange," he said, "and what do these snail things do?"

"Do?"

"Yes, DO. What do they do?"

"Well," Tabbert paused.

Was he thinking or had he seen a bug and was about to go after it? He finally continued. Must have been thinking.

"They each do different things, but, mostly, they're supposed to take care of the garden."

"But, Sage does that," Clawed said.

"No, I mean they're supposed to take care of it from the inside out."

"What does that mean?" Clawed pressed my lips together in a think line.

Tabbert answered. "Suppose you had to wash your fur
44

from the inside. That's what they would do."

Clawed couldn't imagine washing his fur from the inside out, what with the blood and intestines and all. "Hey Tabbert, yesterday I met this group of lizards that hadn't washed for days. Can you imagine the skink?" He'd been brushing up on lizard jokes.

"Haha! That's a good one, Clawed." Tabbert chattered on. "And, according to Lil, the Blinglings have been getting lazy lately. They're not paying attention to the garden. They're preparing for the lottery drawing instead."

"What lottery?" He'd seen those ads on TV. People got all excited about that kind of thing. Somehow, it didn't seem like shiny creatures that moved like snails would want or even need all that money you could win in a lottery.

"Honestly, Clawed, don't you know *anything*?" Clearly agitated, Tabbert skittered around the gutter spout.

Miffed at Tabbert for suggesting that he might be dumb, Clawed looked up at the sky. "Well, excuuuuse me! I know why your tail breaks off so easily. If something is chasing you and grabs you by the tail, it breaks off. Then, it wriggles in the path right where it fell off. It's supposed to distract your pursuer, thereby giving you an opportunity to get away." He'd learned that little fact on Nat Geo.

"Okay, sorry! Anyway, the lottery is a way for the Blinglings to win a prize, but first they have to compete for a ticket."

"How do they get a ticket?"

Tabbert twitched, spun in a circle, dashed up the gutter spout, caught a bug, and raced back. He came to a screeching halt in front of Clawed's nose. "I'm so excited, I can't see straight. The Blinglings compete in contests for the prettiest, the fastest, the strongest, yadda, yadda. The winner of each competition gets a ticket. At the end of the fair, there's a drawing. The holder of the matching numbers wins a prize."

"What kind of prize?" Clawed asked.

"A treasure piece!"

Clawed bit his cheek to contain the sneer sneaking up the right side of his face. Things that glided, washing themselves from the inside out. And now, lottery tickets for treasure pieces.

"It's all new this year! Lay-Z, came up with the idea. He's a camel.

"A camel. In Florida?"

"Yes, a camel. All kinds of creatures live in Bling." He babbled on. "Lil doesn't think the lottery is such a great idea. She says folks should concentrate less on the treasure and more

46

on protecting the garden." Tabbert's tail switched back and forth. He thrust his dewlap out and spun.

Clawed got dizzy watching him.

"I think competing for a treasure piece is a great idea."

"Where are these treasure pieces?"

"In the treasure chest."

"Where is it?"

Tabbert paused and tapped the side of his nose, "Hmmm … I'm not sure…I think it's in the pond, because the Dilitz maids protect it, and they're in the pond."

"Have you ever seen this treasure chest?"

"No." Tabbert answered.

A camel in the garden; and now, a treasure chest. Tabbert was asking him to believe in fairy tales! He truly wanted to. Why couldn't he?

Clawed persisted. "Then, how do you know it's there?"

"Piggy Pomp told me; Lay-Z told her," Tabbert answered quickly, "and Piggy wouldn't lie. There *is* a treasure chest buried down by the pond, or in the it, or somewhere…" His voice faltered. "First of all, you have to go through the rose arbor…"

The rose arbor again. Clawed glanced out the screen at it. A bit scraggly, nothing special, and all those thorns; only a few blooms, and droopy at that.

Tabbert jabbered on. "… past the blueberry flax, follow the cobbled path through the garden, get to the pond and, …uh" Tabbert cleared his throat, looked away, clearly not wanting to meet my eyes, "touch the water."

"Touch the water? Like, with your foot or something?" Suddenly feeling as if it were wet, Clawed examined his paw and licked it.

"Yes, that's right." Tabbert gestured with two of his tong-like toes as if touching the surface of something. "Then, sit back and wait."

Tabbert rushed on without giving Clawed a chance to respond. "You have to create a ripple. The ripple is like... a sound wave. Then you wait, and maybe one of the Dilitz maids comes, or maybe one doesn't. The Dilitz maids are … what can I say? They're particular. Yes, that's it. They're particular… and peculiar. If you want to know anything about the treasure chest, you have to ask one of them. So, you touch the water. That's the signal that somebody wants to talk to them." Tabbert paused to take a breath.

"What exactly is a treasure piece?"

Tabbert paused.

"Do you even know?" Clawed asked.

Tabbert fidgeted, scooted around the gutter spout, and froze.

"Tabbert!"

"Huh? Oh, yeah. I've heard different things. Piggy Pomp said something the other day when we were talking about the fair."

"Don't change the subject. What is a treasure piece?" One cat's trash was another cat's treasure, or so he'd heard. Clawed shuddered to think what Tikky might perceive as treasure.

Tabbert stood and reached his front legs upward as if praising God, or the clouds, or something. His eyes sparkled. "It's a rare and beautiful thing! Something you dream about, a marvel so lovely it brings tears to your eyes. A magical thing."

Holy catfish, was that ever corny. "What does that even mean?" Tabbert loved to be overly dramatic. "And, I'm supposed to believe this because..."

"Er...because that's what Piggy Pomp told me, and she's my friend." Tabbert's eyes closed to slits. He remained very still and stood that way for a while, breathing shallowly, hardly at all, almost like he was in a trance.

"Tabbert." The ornery little lizard still didn't move. Clawed called his name again, louder this time. "Tabbert!"

His eyes sprang open. "I'll be back." He dashed down the

gutter spout, ran across the opening to the rose arbor, and, in a blink, was gone.

"Hmph." Clawed jumped off the ledge and sauntered into the house, climbed onto the back of the couch behind Ben, and settled down for some *Gold Rush* TV. There was no way he could sleep. Gidget looked up at him from the opposite end of the couch. He doubted she had any idea what was going on.

He couldn't picture what Tabbert was describing, let alone believe it. Were there other worlds in the yard besides what he could see? If only he could get back outside.

Chapter 8

Tabbert ran under the rose arbor,

along the cobbled path, then past Blinglings sleeping in the shade. At the water's edge, he stopped and took a deep breath.

He'd never done this before. He couldn't tell that to Clawed though. Suppose what he thought he knew wasn't really true?

Pink and purple bougainvillea bracts waved gently in the breeze. Monarch butterflies danced around the red and orange blooms of their favorite milkweed plants. What a great day to be out in the garden. Poor Clawed, stuck inside.

Tabbert peered into the water, stretching closer and closer to see into the depths, which, according to Piggy, hid the secret treasure chest. His reflection gazed back. "Nice. I'm blue. No wait. Now I'm white. Clawed was right. I *do* change colors in here."

He took a deep breath and glanced over his shoulder. He dabbed at the water with two toes, stepped back, and waited. That's what Piggy had told him to do to call the Dilitz Maids; because the only way to get to the treasure chest was with their assistance. Gentle ripples rolled to the opposite shore.

Becoming drowsier by the minute, he watched, and waited, then waited some more.

Reflecting off the water's rippling surface, the sun blasted a brilliant ray into Tabbert's face. He shielded his eyes and shook to wake himself.

Tabbert touched the surface again, this time with a rear foot. Blinded by the sun, he lost his balance and fell, tail over nose, into the water.

Although he could, Tabbert didn't like to swim. Lickety-split, he turned to scoot out of the water.

But the Dilitz maids were quicker.

Two grabbed Tabbert as he was about to step out of the water. They spun him around and dove, towing him along with them. They hesitated briefly while another secured a bubble around his head so he could breathe. They swam on. For once, Tabbert was speechless.

Although he had believed the Dilitz maids existed, he had never seen one. They had a face of a beluga whale, an hourglass body, and four waving tentacles instead of arms attached to each side. Their translucent, iridescent skin shimmered like moonlight on water, but unlike the Blinglings' crisp lines and facets, they were as smooth as jellyfish.

"Wow, you guys!" Although Tabbert's lips formed the words, no sound came out.

"Hey!" Still no sound. "HEY!!!" He tried again.

The Dilitz maids kept swimming. With tentacles clamped around Tabbert's front legs, they sped through the water at a dizzying pace.

More curious than afraid, Tabbert was thrilled. He was on a mission; and that was perfectly okay with him.

The swim ended abruptly in a spacious, glimmering cavern. The third Dilitz maid removed the bubble surrounding his head, while the two that had dragged him through the water clung to his front legs.

He gasped deeply, as if starved for air, and found that he could still breathe. He stood very still, only rotating his eyes. The Dilitz maids floated, motionless by his sides. Even their tentacles had stopped waving.

Tabbert surveyed his surroundings. The underwater cavern was so clear it was hard to tell what was holding the water back; but something was. Glass? There were no angles, no corners. It was more like a dome. Outside it, shadowy forms drifted by. He suddenly felt like an ant under a glass cake-plate cover.

I'm not afraid. That was a good mantra to repeat. *I'm not afraid.*

He didn't see an entrance. That was a good thing. Those shadows couldn't get in; but how would he get out?

A soft blue light illuminated the room; and even though Tabbert couldn't see the source, the light seemed to come from beyond the chamber's apex. It spun lazily in a way that made him dizzy.

The light swirled above a gleaming chest that hovered inches above the translucent floor; Tabbert couldn't really tell where the floor ended and the walls or the ceiling began. Rainbow-colored rays reflecting off the chest's facets danced around the room.

He fixed his gaze onto the chest.

A voice boomed. "Why are you here?"

Tabbert reeled in a circle. His tail swiped across the faces of the Dilitz maids, broke off, and writhed like a worm on the floor. One Dilitz maid picked it up and held it while the other reattached it to Tabbert's bottom with a sticky bubble it spat from its mouth.

He flicked his tail from side to side. "Wow, cool. Instant tail."

The voice demanded once again. "Why are you here?"

Tabbert looked around. No one else was in the cavern but the Dilitz maids. Earlier, they'd seemed to communicate with a series of clicks and whistling. But he'd heard a human voice. Hadn't he?

He relaxed a bit, took a deep breath, and straightened his spine. "I want to know what's in the treasure chest."

"See for yourself."

The light stopped swirling, and a blue glow filled the room. Tabbert examined himself. Even his skin was blue.

The cavern was silent and still. The chest floated as if it had a life of its own.

Was he dreaming? He pinched himself. Ouch! Yup, he could feel that. Probably not dreaming, he decided.

"Umm, okay." He waited for a long time, unmoving, not even a flick of his tail. There were no more words.

The Dilitz maids remained motionless.

Tabbert placed a foot on his heart. "Still beating," he said. "Just checking. I'm okay. Thank you." Silence.

"I'm okay," he said again with more fortitude than he felt. Still, no voice. "All-righty then! 'See for yourself,' you said.

So, here goes. I'll just have look for myself."

After another quick glance around, he took one step toward the treasure chest. Nothing happened. No swirling lights, no loud voices. He glanced back over his shoulder at the Dilitz maids. They didn't bat an eye or wave a single tentacle. He took another step and paused. He heard Lil's voice in his head. 'Think before reacting, Tabbert.'

He sat back. "Hmm. What do I know? Supposedly, the Dilitz maids are guardians of the treasure, and here they are, like Piggy said they'd be."

The Dilitz maids floated in mid-air like frozen pillars of ice.

"And, there's the treasure chest. So, it's all good, right?" Tabbert tapped his cheek with a scaly toe. "What could go wrong?"

Then, Tabbert remembered what Piggy Pomp had told him about the lottery. "A treasure piece is the prize," she'd said.

He clapped. "I get to see the prize! Maybe it's supposed to be mine. That's why I'm here. I'm in the right place at the right time!"

Tabbert whirled several times. "It's all true! I sent the ripple for the Dilitz maids to come. They did. They brought me to the treasure chest. Everything is just as Piggy told me. I asked to see. I've been shown. That's all there is to it."

He took another step, and then another, until he was so close to the chest, he could touch it. As he reached out to lift the lid, it slowly opened on its own. He jumped back. Sparkling colors and blurry forms became more defined as the lid opened to a 90° angle and stopped. He inched forward until he could clearly see what was inside.

Jewels! Dazzling colors in all shapes and sizes. Drawn to them, Tabbert wanted to touch one. He reached out…

"Messenger!"

"Agk!!!" Tabbert jumped a foot off the floor. Landing on his back legs, he brushed at his chest as if straightening a wrinkled suit. "Whew, you startled me."

"Take one!"

The lizard spun. His rotating eyes observed every inch of the room, searching for the source of the voice. The Dilitz maids stood lifeless as before. The voice had come from behind him, beside him, from all around him.

Tabbert used his most commanding tone. "You gotta quit doing that. Who are you anyway?"

"Take one!" the voice repeated.

"No, no, that's okay." Tabbert backed away. "I didn't come to take anything. Really! I only wanted to know what was *in* the chest."

"Take one," the voice commanded. "Then you will know."

"No, really, it's okay," Tabbert said. "I can see what's in there. And, they're beautiful too, yes they are." Slowly, he continued backing away.

"Take one!!!"

"Okay!" Tabbert crept toward the chest and reached inside.

It was not a decision that later on he remembered deliberately making. It was as if, by magic, one particular red gem jumped into his tong-like toes. He now held one glittering jewel, and inside it whirled a living amalgamation of colors.

He gazed deep into the shimmering sunset pinks and spinning threads of gold all swimming in a sea of crimson crystal.

At the same time that the lid began to close with the smooth silence by which it had opened, the jewel began to grow.

"Huh!" Tabbert tried to put it back, but found that he couldn't let go of it. It almost seemed that his toes wrapped more tightly around it. The gem grew larger until he had to put it down. It was too heavy to hold.

When it reached almost half Tabbert's body size, he shook

a clenched foot toward the ceiling. "What in the world?"

"Tabbert," the Voice said. "Take it with you!"

"Yeah, yup, okay!" Tabbert's tail flicked back and forth. His head bobbed. His body twitched. Excited to the maximum level his lizard body could possibly take, Tabbert strained to pick up the jewel.

"Grrrrrrgh!" It didn't budge. He pressed his shoulder against it and shoved with all his might. It still didn't move.

"Take it with me? Uh huh…sure. And *how* am I supposed to do that?" He frowned, worry furrows deepening between his eyes, then tried again. "Eeeooowwrrrgh!" Had it moved, even an inch? "How heavy is this thing anyway?"

"You wanted to know, you wanted to see, and so you have. Now, TAKE IT WITH YOU."

A firm voice, indeed, but somehow not as intimidating anymore. Tabbert took a deep breath and scowled. "You know, whoever you are…this is a bit irritating."

"Yes, it is."

With his hands on his hips and his chin jutting out, Tabbert walked around the gem. "I don't know how I'm going to move that thing."

"Then, you will stay until you figure it out."

"You've got to be kidding."

59

"No, I'm not." The light dimmed. "And, Tabbert?

"Yes?" Tabbert's muscles quivered.

"You will do this. I'm positive of that."

"Hmph."

Tabbert slumped to the floor like a deflated balloon. That voice, whoever or whatever it was, might be sure of that, but Tabbert wasn't. He wished he'd never reached out to the Dilitz maids in the first place, wished he were back on his gutter down-spout minding his own business, wished he could think of a joke that would lighten the moment. But he couldn't think of anything to joke about.

Clawed was stuck inside.

Who was going to save him now?

Chapter 9

Tree Huggers are green

and some people are tree huggers. Sage hugged trees sometimes, and Tabbert said she's green.

To Clawed she appeared a bit gray, but then, he couldn't see all the colors of the spectrum. Tabbert could. As a matter of fact, reptiles could see all the colors humans do and more. Who knew; maybe Sage was green.

Clawed had never seen a green person. That didn't mean they don't exist. He was questioning himself again. Since Tabbert had come into his life, he'd been questioning a lot of things.

Like—Blinglings? Clawed could hardly picture them.

Cats were the most normal species he knew. They took care of themselves, washed without being told, and didn't submit to treat-induced commands like 'sit,' 'roll over,' or 'give me your paw.' Pathetic.

Tabbert hadn't been around for a couple of days. Clawed had taken a liking to the little critter and hoped nothing had happened to him. Where was he?

Clawed patted Ben's arm. "Hey." He was reading the paper and watching the news on TV at the same time. "I need to tell you something."

Ben scratched Clawed's head in such a namby-pamby way, Clawed wasn't sure he even knew he was there. He took a bite out of Ben's newspaper and meowed.

"No, Clawed. Here, read this." Ben placed the comics section over him.

Ordinarily, Clawed would have liked the hiding place Ben had created, but he was worried. He arched his back. The newspaper slid to the floor. He leapt onto Ben's lap, onto the end table, then jumped to the floor.

"Hey, quit that," Ben said.

"Later," Clawed meowed. "I'm going to find Sage, maybe she'll listen." He gave Ben a quick twitch of his tail and left the room without a backward glance.

When he couldn't find Sage, he exited the house through the cat door that led out to the back patio and climbed to the top of his tower, the perfect lookout from which to observe the back yard.

Sage was humming somewhere in the side yard. She came into view, weeding here, pruning there, inspecting this wilted blossom, and frowning over some droopy greenery.

"Sage!"

"Hi, Clawed. What're you doing, big guy?"

"I need to talk to you." He scratched at the screen.

"Don't do that." She waggled a finger at him.

"But…Tabbert's been gone for a while. Keep your eye out for him, will you?"

Clawed sighed and retracted his claws. He hated being stuck inside.

Sage worked her way around to the back yard. A summer breeze blew her long, silvery hair around her shoulders. How could she work in the garden all afternoon without a nap?

Clawed looked more closely at the garden. The bougainvillea seemed more gangly than usual, the milkweed scraggly and losing its leaves. The yellow-faced pansies drooped like sad children, and the rose's dead branches needed pruning.

He hadn't noticed it before. Sage's hard work didn't seem to be helping. The flowers were sparse, the branches almost bare. What was wrong?

Sage approached the rose arbor and gasped softly.

Clawed jumped down from his carpeted platform, then jumped up on the knee-wall ledge closest to her to get a better look.

She cupped a pink rose in her hand. Its center appeared dry and shriveled and was turning black like it was decaying from within. The ruffled edges of the petals were withered, curling inward, shrinking toward the flower's heart. Moist droplets of red clung to the tips of the thorns, like the flower was bleeding!

A tear rolled down Sage's cheek, fell onto a petal, and slid into the center of the rose.

For a brief moment, the black faded, and the rose was restored. Huh? He blinked.

Within a breath's time, the rose withered again. Right before Clawed's eyes. Had he fallen asleep; was he having the strangest nightmare of his life? He licked his paw and rubbed his eyes.

He thought about the other day when he and Tabbert had

64

been having a passionate discussion about colors of things.

 "Sage and Ben aren't really green," Clawed had said. "That's only a figure of speech."

Tabbert cocked his head. "Green? I'm green, um… most of the time anyway." He tapped his chest. "I didn't say they were green as in skin green. They don't look green to me either. More like pink—ish."

"Pink? You don't know everything. *I* read the paper…"

"From what I see," Tabbert interrupted defensively, "you *eat* the paper."

"I don't eat the paper."

"Then, what are you doing when you're shredding it with those daggers of yours."

"Are you going to listen? And how do you know what I eat anyway?"

Tabbert said he often snuck into the house, but kept to the shadows whenever he came inside. He wasn't a hundred percent sure Gidget wouldn't leave him tail-less, or worse, eat him.

"Okay, okay," Tabbert took a deep breath. "I was just saying, they don't look green to me."

Clawed continued his lecture. "I mean, they care about the

environment. That's why they're called tree huggers, and that's synonymous with *green*."

"Yeah, yeah. I get it."

But Clawed could hear the doubt in his voice. Tabbert didn't know that Sage and Ben didn't use pesticides like the neighbors did. That was the worst. Talk about respiratory infection. No telling what other ills the chemicals caused.

Clawed went on. "You know those brown anoles—the ones you don't like?   Ben rescues them. And he saves cockroaches and spiders too. 'Everything has the right to live,' he says."

"And when Sage and Ben go back inside," Tabbert said, "the brown lizards, spiders, and bugs eat each other; but hey, what do I know."

Clawed ignored Tabbert's obvious sarcasm and repeated what he'd learned on the Green Planet channel. "We've got to take care of the earth, it's our home. The environment gets sick, we get sick."

Tabbert's tail twitched back and forth. "Right! It's like I've been telling you! That's what the Blinglings are supposed to do; take care of the garden, from the inside out. Lil tells them all the time, 'can't have pretty flowers if the roots aren't fed, can't grow strong roots if the water and soil are poor.'"

"Yay, you *do* get it!"

Clawed and Tabbert high-fived through the screen. Then Clawed sat back, satisfied with the quiet comfort of the afternoon.

Friends who understood each other was a good thing.

Thinking of Tabbert, Clawed frowned and sat up. Where was he anyway?

"MMMRRRRROWWWWW!!!"

Clawed about jumped out of his skin. The fur on his hackles stood straight up.

"MMMRRRROWWWWW!!!" again.

"What the…?" A movement at his side drew his attention away from Sage and what had just happened in the garden.

Gidget was sitting right there on the ledge next to him. It was just like her to sneak up on him. Why, oh, why did she cry like that?

"Did you see that?" Clawed asked. "Huh? Did you? I've got to tell Tabbert! He's been saying something's wrong with the garden."

"Mmrrrowww." Gidget meowed quieter this time.

"Shush!" Clawed stood on the ledge.

Everything Tabbert had been saying was beginning to

make sense in some convoluted, crazy, sort of way. Clawed was pretty certain Gidget had seen what he'd seen.

What had he seen?

"You know," he said turning away from her, "it would be nice if instead of crying, you'd talk for once."

Being cooped up inside and trying to understand all this magic stuff was making him grouchy. He climbed to the top of his tower and didn't come down until supper.

Previously...

Chapter 10

Gidget's Second Life

and third, and fourth were as dangerous as her first.

Hidden by the lengthening forest shadows, the gray tabby kitten fell asleep, then woke two more times to nurse while Mother Cat continued to sleep. Finally, the kitten fell into a deep slumber.

Under the cover of darkness, Mother Cat ran with a firm hold of the scruff of her baby's neck in her teeth.

She made it to a safe shelter as the sun was beginning to rise.

The kitten awoke suddenly. The sunny spot she'd been dreaming about had been replaced by a musty odor that made her sneeze. When she caught her breath, she found herself practically buried under a mound of hay. Hackles raised and teeth bared, Mother Cat stood over her like a radiator hissing on overload.

Strange cats surrounded the intruders: fat ones, tabbies-some orange, some gray, fluffy ones, black and white ones; curious kittens huddled warily behind them.

A large calico snarled in her face. "Who are you?"

A skinny, white Persian growled at her.

Mother Cat hissed. "Back off!" She lashed out at the Persian, her sharp claws barely missing its whiskers. Mother Cat was a seasoned warrior, and nothing, not even a dozen barn cats, could scare her. It had been a difficult couple of days. She was not in a good mood.

A smaller, orange female with a placid face approached slowly. "You surprised us, is all. My name—"

"Stay away…" Mother hissed again.

 "Step back, you guys!" A droopy-eyed horse stomped its huge hoof. "Give her some breathing room."

Cats scattered in all directions, except for Mother and her kitten. "Calm down, little mama." Big Nel lowered her head. "Pretty baby girl you've got there."

Mother swiped at the horse's nose.

Nel tossed her head back. "Whoa there, feisty lady.

70

Nobody's going to hurt you. I'll make sure of that. They're curious, is all. You settle down. I'll be right here."

Nel turned her towering body to the wall and planted her hooves around the mother and her kitten. She glared at the clutter of cats. "I dare you to come one step closer." None did.

Little by little, the fur along Mother Cat's back smoothed out, and, bone weary, she slowly relaxed.

The kitten huddled close and nuzzled her mother for another meal.

But Mother Cat hadn't eaten since the altercation with Leroy. How long ago was that? And, when had she eaten before that? There was no milk. The kitten cried.

Mother Cat licked her. "It'll be okay." She purred to the hungry baby. "You have to wait a bit."

Mother wanted to sleep. She was so tired. But she still had to feed her kitten but didn't know where to get food.

"Hey! Horse!"

The horse was snoring.

"Hmph, 'I'll be right here.' Yeah right." Mother nudged her kitten further into the hay. "You stay right there. I have to find dinner. I won't be long."

The kitten cried. "Nooooooo!" Mother had left so many times before. Those waits could be horribly long. "No, please, meeeowww, please!"

"Hush!" Mother Cat boxed the kitten's ear. "You want to eat?"

The kitten hunkered down in the hay and whimpered. "I want to go with you."

"You're not big enough. Now, stay quiet. And don't move."

Mother didn't come back all that day. As the light in the barn grew dimmer, a tantalizing aroma woke her. The kitten's stomach growled. "Mother!"

Smelling of oats and grass, Nel nudged through the hay and found the kitten. "You still here?" Looking around, Nel asked, "Where's your mother? Off hunting, I suppose. Too bad she didn't know she could've had something to eat right here.

"Hungry, are you?" Nel lowered her head and gently grasped the kitten with her front teeth like she'd seen the barn cats do with their kittens. Clip, clop, clopping across the wide plank floor, she carried the kitten to the feed dish Hudson put out for the cats, and dropped her by it.

The barn cats complained. "Hissssss!!! SSSSSSSSSSSS!!! Meeeeeowwww."

"Oh, hush," Nel said. "This little gal ain't gonna hurt

anything. Ain't gonna eat much, neither. Let her have some."

Gidget was almost too frightened to eat, but the scent of the food gave her courage. She crept to the lip of the dish, crawled into it, and plowed her face into the pile of mush and kibbles. Soft food plugged her nose and covered her eyes.

She'd never had dry food before. She tried to swallow. A piece stuck in her throat. She gagged and coughed, and sneezed, then gagged again.

A thin, gray tabby coached her. "Slow down, itty bit. One bite at a time."

The kitten coughed more, sneezed again. She wiped the food that clung to her face. She couldn't see, and wiping it with her tiny paw didn't help. The piece of food lodged in her throat made her cough again. Weak from hunger, she lost her breath and fell over.

The white Persian yowled. "Nel! Do something!"

"Tarnation. Doesn't that little thing know how to eat yet?"

"Almighty haystack; do something!"

Nel prodded the kitten with her nose. When the kitten didn't respond, the horse nudged her, not a big nudge, but coming from a horse, it was as if a baseball bat propelled her through the air. The kitten landed three feet away with a plop.

"Oooff!" She coughed, spat out the dry kibble, gasped,

then caught her breath. She stood shakily. Tripping over herself, she made her way back to the food bowl.

Nel nodded her head and smiled. "This one's got guts, don't she?"

The kitten ate one bite at a time. When she was full, she sniffed her way back to mother's scent in the hay and curled up into a ball.

"That's right, little one. Sleep now." Nel returned to her position guarding the kitten's nest.

Baby grew drowsy waiting for Mother and dozed off, but not for long. The barn kittens snuck through the hay and crowded around her.

"Where'd you come from? Where's your mother? Are you staying? What's your name?"

"Mother!" Gidget wailed. She didn't want to make friends. She was tired from her long ordeal. Curled into a quivering lump, she cowered in the corner of Nel's stall.

Farmer Hudson didn't like too many cats in the barn. It was okay to have some. Kept the rat population down, they did. That was the only reason he put a dish of food out for them every day. Well, that, and because the missus insisted.

But if he didn't keep the cat population under control, the

place could get overrun with them. Occasionally, he "managed" the ever-growing cat community.

Next morning, after Hudson fed the menagerie, he told his wife, "I'm going duck hunting."

He took his straw hat from the hook behind the door, slapped it on his head, and grabbed his shotgun from the mantel and an empty burlap feed sack from under the vestibule bench. "Come on, Butch."

He and a chocolate Labrador headed back to the barn. Once there, he clanked Nel's oat scoop on the galvanized pan he used to feed the feral cats.

Conditioned to the sound, cats and kittens tumbled over one another in a hurry to get to the dish. Another meal?

Hudson quickly scooped up three kittens and dropped them into the burlap bag. They tumbled heads over tails to the bottom, their claws catching in the burlap weave.

The thin gray tabby and the white Persian plowed into him, their teeth and claws bared for a fight. He shoved them away with a swift kick.

He picked up four more kittens and dropped them into the bag, too. Nel stood her ground over the Baby. "Get out of the way, you old nag." He nudged Nel aside and found Baby cowering in the hay. "Haven't seen you around before." He put

75

her in the bag with the others and loosely pulled the drawstring.

Neil stomped her feet and nipped his shoulder as he turned to leave.

"It's gotta be done, Old Nel. You know it."

She tossed her head back and whinnied. "Not your way, it doesn't."

The farmer threw the bag over his shoulder. 'Better not bite me again. You might lose the comfort of this here barn."

"Mew mew mew mew;" tiny little squeaks, some loud wails, all heartbreaking cries.

Gun in one hand, burlap sack in the other, Hudson passed through a citrus grove, then crossed to the far end of the hayfield. When he reached a stand of cattails at the edge of the distant cow pond, he spied a flock of mallards swimming out in the open water.

He slowly set the burlap bag down in the shallows, raised his gun, and shot. Ducks flew off in every direction. He pulled the trigger again.

Water seeped into the burlap bag. Frightened by the loud gun shots and the frantic cries of the other kittens, Gidget floundered as the sinking weight of the wet burlap pressed her under the water.

The kittens' desperate struggles loosened the unknotted drawstring. The mouth of the bag gaped open.

Gidget clawed her way out of the bag and found herself in the water. Crying, she tried to swim, grasped nothing with her tiny sharp nails, flailed about, and …

Was she swimming? Something clamped a tight hold on her legs and pushed her out of the water. Fresh air filled her lungs.

When she felt solid ground under her feet, she collapsed in the grass beyond the water's edge.

Weariness settled over her. Deafened by the ringing thunder of the gun and water in her ears, she barely heard the locusts buzzing in the grass. The Dilitz maids quietly slipped away.

Soaking wet and shivering, Gidget crawled to a clump of swamp grass and crouched low in the thick reeds. She struggled to control her ragged breathing while ducks plummeted out of the sky all around her.

To any other kitten it may have seemed like a nightmare. To Gidget, this was life. Hard. Survival was questionable, but for the moment, she was still alive.

Her stomach growled. How was she going to find something to eat? Mother had always done that for her.

Swallowing a sob, she crouched down, trying to make herself as small as possible. "Mother where are you?"

Chapter 11

Tabbert sat staring into the jewel

for a long time. Gold, vein-like threads wound around and through the amber and red-grape-colors that swirled inside the gem's crystalline faceted exterior. It was beautiful and monstrous at the same time.

How had it grown? Was it alive? He peered closer at the gem, his eyes reflected in its gleaming facets.

He glanced around again, wondering if he might locate the source of the Voice. He didn't. He pressed his nose against the cold gemstone.

"Anybody in there?" Pale blue, he stood taut with anticipation, as still as the frozen Dilitz maids. The cavern exuded a crisp energy that gave Tabbert goose bumps. The cold made him sluggish. All was still.

Had he turned into a Blingling?

Barely moving a muscle or twitching a nostril, he waited. Only his eyes rotated as he searched the cavern for a door, something, someone. Nothing. The Dilitz maids hovered nearby, eyes unblinking, tentacles as motionless as pillars of stone.

No more shadows swam in the blue expanse outside the dome. There were no waves or ripples, no bubbles or currents.

Tabbert stifled a yawn. "Can't fall asleep. Gotta keep my wits about me. How am I going to move this thing?" The Dilitz maids offered no sage words of advice. The booming voice gave no instructions.

For the first time in his carefree existence, Tabbert felt trapped. Imprisoned in a blurry, submerged cavern, even the Dilitz maids, stonily statuesque in their guardianship of the gem-filled treasure chest, seemed locked in the transparent embrace of this underwater hold.

Only the jewel, awhirl with color, sparkled before his eyes.

"Hmph. Some treasure. What good is it?" Tabbert's shoulders and eyelids drooped. "What am I doing here?"

He'd been trying to convince Clawed that Bling and the lottery prize were really real. So, he'd gone to ask the Dilitz maids if he could see the treasure chest. "Why should I care about a glass gem?" Then the bigger question came to him. "Why should anyone care?" Lil had been saying it the whole time. All the Blinglings cared about was a dumb treasure piece, and now—look at the garden.

The cold slowed his brain activity, making him groggy and lethargic. As he drifted into a daze, Tabbert thought about Bling, and its sparkling inhabitants, how he was able to come and go—a part of two worlds.

Trapped, with a jewel bigger than anyone could imagine, he was like a silly old ant trying to move a rubber tree plant.

He wished he were back in Bling. He was the Messenger. "I have to tell them. This stupid rock isn't going to help anyone in Bling. Not Piggy Pomp, not…"

"Taa…bbert…" the voice again, softer now.

He spun around so quickly even Clawed's eye might not have detected the movement.

Tabbert was so frustrated, he yelled. "What! Where are you? Show yourself!"

"Tabbert," more softly this time, "you can move the jewel."

"How?" No answer. Tabbert shook a fist at the treasure chest. "I will save Bling. Wait and see."

Chapter 12

Lil-the Secretarycat

and Shep sat together in the shade of the plumbago bush. Its clusters of blueish-violet petals swayed gently in the afternoon breeze.

A monarch flitted from one milkweed flower to the next.

 "Look at her, Lil. She looks like a stained-glass window. Beautiful, isn't she?"

"Um hm…" Lil answered vaguely. "This change won't last for her either. We have to make the most of what we have, here and now. That's what Stocker has told me time and time again."

"You sound like you're trying to convince yourself," Shep said.

Off in the distance, Zodiaq crowed. "Cock-a-doodle-do,

changes come to me and you, cock-a-doodle-do, what are you going to do-oo?"

Lil lifted her face and sniffed the air. "Shep?"

"Yes?"

"It's almost time."

"I know."

"Tabbert's in the treasure cave."

Shep nodded. "Right where our Messenger is supposed to be."

"I don't understand why it has to be this way." Lil backed into the shade of the plumbago bush. "I'm not sure I'm going to like this promotion. This is going to be hard."

"We've been through this before. Change is always hard."

"Yes, and the Blinglings don't listen. They've become self-absorbed, believing their way is best. The new Secretarycat has her work cut out for her."

"Stocker is so patient and forgiving, but he's also wise. Maybe the Blinglings need a tougher task master. You've become quite motherly and more than patient with them. Maybe too patient, hm?"

Lil sighed. She had been Stocker's trusted assistant since... "Why can't I remember?"

"Remember what, Lil?"

"Where I was, what I did before I started working with Stocker. The new secretarycat is coming from somewhere else. I can't remember my somewhere else."

"Why are you asking that?"

"Because Tabbert asked me once, and I couldn't answer. Then he asked me if I knew what *he* did before he became a messenger."

"What did you tell him?"

"I told him to stop wasting my time with a bunch of silly questions and do his job."

"Good advice. And that satisfied him?"

"I guess so. I've only known Tabbert as a messenger, haven't you?" She went on. "Why does everyone come to me? And, this promotion Stocker has been telling me about? What will I be doing? What was I before this? Why can't I remember?"

"Hmm..." Shep paused and watched the monarch flit from flower to flower. "I don't think we're supposed to know everything, Lil. Some things are beyond our understanding. That's where faith comes in."

"Sometimes I feel like we're not appreciated. Why can't the humans see us?" Lil asked.

"They do. They just don't recognize us for what we are

yet, but they might if they look closer." Shep pointed toward the house. "People like Sage and Ben. We're lucky to have them. Makes our job easier. Hmm...maybe too easy?" He scanned the garden. "I sense a change coming out there too. That's why we need Tabbert, remember? You've told him he has to get their attention."

"But, will it be in time? And, what about us? I'm not sure I like the idea that I have to change in order for it to be better for them."

"Have you become like the rest of Bling?" Shep scolded gently. "Don't want to make waves? Stagnation or change, greed or charity, sloth or industry; our choices create life or death in the garden. We are all connected. It's been this way forever."

"Like Stocker always says."

"Mm hm." Shep nodded.

When Lil spoke again, her voice seemed strained. "Are you going to the lottery pick?"

"Of course, Lil. I have to. We both do. Why all these questions?"

Why indeed? Lil had no idea what the upcoming promotion would require of her. She'd been guiding the others for so long she'd forgotten to think about her own life. Things were going to change, and, to be honest, she was afraid.

The monarch flitted away, taking a haphazard, zig-zag flight path.

Like my life, Lil thought. "What if I fail?"

"I promise you, Lil," Shep said. "You won't. We both have jobs to do. I have to choose the Picker, and I still haven't figured out who it's going to be."

Lil sighed. "I'm glad I don't have that responsibility. Whose idea was the fair and the lottery prize, anyway?"

"Probably Stocker's. I'd bet he put the idea in Lay-Z's head. Lay-Z's the one who announced the lottery, and the fair, and Tabbert's birthday."

"That figures; and he isn't even participating." Lil hung her head.

She didn't believe in the whole lottery deal. No matter how often she'd tried to motivate them lately, the Blinglings wouldn't listen. A promotion might be a welcome change.

"I wonder what the new Secretarycat will be like."

"Whoever it is, Stocker will make sure she or he does their job."

Lil nodded. "Oh yeah, you can be sure of that. He's the boss."

Chapter 13

Gidget didn't get too close

to anyone or anything. She'd been shot at, almost eaten by a mangy mongrel, and she had almost drowned. She was afraid, and didn't trust anyone. She'd been hurt too many times.

With claws extended and digging deep, she'd leap away the instant Sage or Ben pulled her too close or hugged her too hard.

What Gidget lacked in trust she made up for in determination. She had a good sixth sense and an uncanny way of knowing...something's up.

It was a day or so after Tabbert had gone missing.

Gidget must have been feeling talkative all of a sudden and roused Clawed from a nap he was taking on the couch.

"Hey…pssst." Her voice cracked like she needed a drink of water. "I need to go outside."

Sage and Ben had put the k-bosh on that one. Didn't she remember?

She boxed his ears. "Clawed!"

"What!" He opened his eyes and yawned. "You need to relax," he told her. "Like me."

"You know what, Clawed? You think you'll always be fed," she said. "…that you'll always have someplace dry and warm to sleep, and that Sage and Ben will keep you safe. But life isn't always like that. Stuff happens, and being a pampered couch potato is only for the rich and famous, or the fat and lazy, like you."

He choked on that. "Chill out, Gidget. Who are you to tell me what I think? Things are going to be okay, so quit worrying; it isn't helping. And besides that, I'm not lazy. I'm conserving my energy for...whenever I need it." He just rarely needed it.

"Whatever." She cleared her throat, then coughed as if she were bringing up a hairball. "I wanted to tell you. I did see that."

"See what?"

"I saw what happened to that flower the other day when

88

Sage's tear dropped into its center. The black went away."

"You saw that?" Clawed was wide awake now and sat up.

Gidget nodded. "And I saw Tabbert disappear too."

"You did?"

"And…"

He waited forever for her to continue.

Finally, she spoke again. "I know about the magic."

"You do?" He jumped off the couch. "Let's go out to the back porch. We've got some talking to do."

They jumped onto the ledge near Tabbert's gutter spout. The sunny afternoon felt steamy and hot. Hopefully, that meant it would rain soon. The weatherman was still talking about the drought.

Sage was outside snipping, pruning, and weeding out invasive species that she said choked out the native plants.

A fine dust drifted through the screen from the construction site next door. Gidget sneezed, then cried. "Mmrrrowww!"

"What are you crying about now?" Clawed asked.

"What I'm always crying about. I'm worried for *all* the plants. Remember how that flower withered again right after the black went away? Clawed, something weird is happening."

Sage gathered up her pile of withered blooms and

browning brush and headed toward the compost pile. She'd probably dig a hole and bury it along with the day-old cucumber peels, potato skins, and used coffee grounds.

She walked past the rose arbor. It seemed like the blossoms raised their heads, or maybe Clawed imagined it, because in the next instant, they seemed droopy again.

Clawed looked over his shoulder rather than look into Gidget's frightened eyes.

If Gidget already knew what Tabbert had been trying to tell him about all this time, maybe Bling really did exist. And Lil was real, and Piggy Pomp too, which probably meant the lottery was real. The garden was obviously sick, and only God knew what was going to happen next.

"How long have you known?" Clawed asked.

"Since before I came here."

"Have you seen the Blinglings?"

She nodded.

"Really? Care to tell me about it?"

"Um...okay."

"Come on, we'll talk up on my cat tower."

"*Your* cat tower. Oh. Okay."

Clawed chose to ignore the slight sneer she gave him. Gidget hadn't talked this much the entire time she'd lived here.

He tucked his legs beneath him and settled onto the top level of the tower. She sat on the one below him.

Maybe she could make sense of all the weird things going on. If only Tabbert could hear this. Where was he?

Chapter 14

Gidget's Fifth Life

was as hard as her previous ones.

Alone, wet, and shivering, she crouched low in the grass, her breath ragged, her heart pounding. Her ears still rang from the thunder of Farmer Hudson's gun. She coughed up the last bit of water left in her lungs, ridding her body of the fluid that had almost stolen her last breath.

Something had pushed her out of the water. Where were the other kittens? She looked around. None were nearby. With her ears tuned for cries, she lightly dozed while the sun warmed and dried her fur.

She dreamt of a cavern with watery blue light and jelly-like creatures with huge rounded faces, hourglass bodies, and waving tentacles, their translucent skin reflecting rainbows and shimmering like diamonds.

The dream changed, and she found herself tangled in thorny branches covered with black roses. The more she struggled to get free, the deeper the thorns stuck into her.

Her blood dripped onto the ground. Fresh seedlings burst forth from the ground beneath the tangled thicket. As suddenly as the seedlings grew, they died.

Gidget awoke, too frightened to move. Where was Mother? She shuddered when the reeds and cattails crackled around her.

Sneaking along behind him, eleven-year-old Meg Hudson had often followed her father. She understood why he did what he did, but she didn't like it, not one bit; and this time she aimed to do something about it.

As soon as her father left the pond, Meg searched the area where he'd dumped the burlap bag. She found Gidget, scooped her up and held the kitten to her chest.

"Quit fidgeting, little kitty. I'm only trying to help." Wrapping the kitten inside her favorite, yellow sweater, she searched the surrounding grass and cattails. She located two more kittens. Holding them with Gidget in her sweater, she

93

headed to a clearing in the pine forest where she and her friends had dug a fire pit and encircled it with stones.

She unwrapped the kittens. "What am I going to do with you now?" She couldn't bring them home. Looking around, she spied a grocery cart that had been in the woods for a long time. "Maybe I can use that."

She yanked at vines that had grown around and through the woven steel until she freed the cart. She set it upright, then placed the kittens inside it.

They stumbled as their tiny legs fell through the holes in the woven steel bottom.

Meg tore up a box she'd recently brought into the woods for fire starter, set the cardboard in the bottom of the cart, then lay her sweater over it. "There you go."

Mom would scold her for not bringing her sweater home. Did she think money grew on trees, that she could just leave her sweater lying about?

Meg would have to return to the woods to get it. It would give her a chance to come back with food for the kittens.

She ripped another piece of cardboard off the box and folded it in half for a tent-like cover, then picked them up, naming each one as she did.

"You're awfully squirmy. I'll call you Gidget to rhyme

with fidget." She smoothed the gray tabby's fur, then petted the orange tabby. "I'll call you Tikky because you don't seem to be afraid of anything. And, I'll call you Daisy," she said to the third, "because you're a calico just like the one I used to have.

"See you in a while." She placed the cover over them and left.

For a long time, Gidget stared through the wire cart at the woods Meg disappeared into. The others meowed, sniffed one another, and cried. Gidget was exhausted and hungry.

She'd been hungry before. All her short life that was all she'd been doing; waiting for food. She scratched at the sweater and rumpled it into a pile. Eventually, the other kittens curled up next to her. Strange as they were, their closeness offered some comfort.

Meg wasn't allowed to come back later. She'd have to get her sweater tomorrow.

No food or water for the rest of that exhausting day sapped the kittens of what little strength they had. As day passed into night, sounds coming out of the dark frightened her, but she remained quiet. Mother had taught her that. She instinctively slowed her breathing, and, with the other kittens, slipped into a state of semi-consciousness.

At dawn, a noisy green bird screeched from the branch overhead. "It's morning. Get up!"

Weak, Gidget pulled herself around the cart, sniffed at every fold in the sweater. Hunger pains tore at her stomach. Daisy cried. Tikky yowled.

Gidget slept again, dreaming of the barn where she'd had her last meal, then of a fairground where rainbow-colored creatures danced and laughed.

The scene shifted and she dreamed of running, soggy ground opening up and swallowing her. The day passed into another night with no food, just the yellow sweater with a fading smell of the human who had captured them and put them in this cold, steel cell.

Gidget huddled against the others, finding comfort in them and giving back as much as she took.

Morning light blinded the kittens as it suddenly beamed into their faces.

"Oh, kitties." Meg held them briefly before putting them back down on the sweater.

"You must be starving." She opened a can and spooned it

onto a paper plate, then poured milk from a single serving carton she'd purchased at the 7-Eleven and set the dish on the floor of the cart.

"I'm sorry I left you out here for so long." One by one, Gidget first, she gently placed each kitten by the edge of the dish.

With wobbly legs, they crowded onto the plate. Gidget coughed as she ate. Tikky snorted as he gobbled. Daisy lapped quietly. They ate every morsel, then licked each other's fur until every bit of food was gone.

***

"You could have starved to death!" Clawed said.

Gidget jumped off the ledge to get a drink from the pool. Here at Sage and Ben's, she would never be without water again.

She settled back onto the ledge. "Yes...but, I couldn't think about that." Her voice cracked from talking so much. "I had to survive, even if all I could do was breathe one minute at a time. I was just grateful I was still alive."

Clawed looked out the screen. "All this time, you were right out there in those woods?" He gestured toward the north tree line that separated the cul-de-sac from Farmer Hudson's farm. "I went in those woods before..." Clawed cleared his throat, then swiped his whiskers clean. "…before I hurt my foot."

Gidget interrupted. "About that…"

"What?"

"The day you chased that orange mess of a tomcat out of the yard?"

"Yeah, what about it?"

"I know him."

"Oh, really?" Clawed looked away, embarrassed that she'd witnessed the incident.

"Tikky was one of the other cats in the shopping cart with me. He's had a hard time."

"Whatever." Gidget seemed to be friends with the one cat who irritated Clawed to no end. "I don't care about him. What kind of a name is that for a cat anyway? Tikky tacky. I think he's wacky."

Clawed didn't want to talk about him. He changed the subject.

"So, how do you know about the garden?" He asked.

"I'm getting to that."

"I'm really feeling like a nap," Clawed replied, but stayed right where he was.

Chapter 15

Gidget cried in her sleep

almost every night. She missed Mother even though the warm memory of her was beginning to dim. Daisy's snuggling gave her the comfort she needed so badly. Tikky flopped on top of them despite their complaints that he was getting too heavy for that.

That afternoon, Meg had taken the kittens out of the cart to play on a thick bed of pine needles. They were growing stronger and more curious by the day.

After Meg left, Gidget had a strong urge to explore some more. "Let's see if we can climb out of this thing."

Tikky was immediately interested.

Daisy wasn't. "No, no, no," she cried. "We might not be able to get back in."

"So what?" Gidget shoved a paw through a hole in the steel weave of the cart wall, then put another paw in a hole above that one and pulled herself up. "It's easy!" She pushed with her hind legs. One foot after the other, she slowly climbed to the top of the cart and teetered there until she fell over the side onto the ground.

"Ooof." She meowed, shook herself, and got to her feet. "Come on, Tikky."

"No, Tikky. Don't," said Daisy.

"Don't be a chicken." Tikky copied Gidget, and pulled himself out of the cart. He landed on the ground with a thump, an ooof, and a shake, none the worse for the fall.

Daisy peered out at the two cats on the ground. "I'm not coming."

"Your loss," Tikky said.

Gidget and Tikky scrambled across the clearing, clawed their way over logs, tumbled into the fire pit, and wrestled in the cold ashes. They soon grew tired of playing. Curious about what was beyond the clearing, they agreed to explore farther.

Daisy called after them. "Where are you guys going?

Don't go far. How will you get back in?"

They ignored her. Such interesting smells; mole tracks, lizard tails, leaping grasshoppers!

"Hey, I can catch that bug." Tikky pounced but missed a bee that buzzed by. Gidget swiped at a brown Cuban lizard and caught nothing but air in her claws. This was fun. Their frolicking carried them farther and farther away from the shopping cart.

They barely heard Daisy yelling. "Come back!"

Gidget and Tikky stopped at the edge of the wood thicket and peered into the orange grove where the grass grew high over their heads.

"We better go back," Gidget said, wary now.

"Not yet." Tikky ran out into the tall grass.

"Wait." Gidget leapt in front of him. "It's almost suppertime."

Tikky pushed past her and scampered after a dragonfly. "Watch this!" He gathered his legs beneath his belly and leapt for the darting insect. He missed by a mile. Gidget laughed.

"Hey, look." A voice came from the branches over their heads. "A kitten!"

"Look, there's another one," voiced another. Two boys scrambled down from the tree.

Gidget froze.

Tikky ran to the nearest tree and climbed. The boys couldn't follow him there. One tried, but couldn't climb as high as Tikky had.

The other caught Gidget. "Aww, cute kitty."

Ignoring Tikky up in the tree, the boys handed Gidget back and forth, petting her, and lifting her up in the air until she was sure she'd be sick.

"I'm gonna take her home, see if my mom will let me keep her."

"She's not gonna let you."

"Maybe she will."

"She won't."

The boy put Gidget in the Sweet Crunchies cereal box they'd been snacking out of and left the clearing with his friend.

Tikky stayed in the tree top all night.

Daisy cried herself to sleep. Meg had not come with supper. Tikky and Gidget didn't come back either.

In a new home with strange sounds and even stranger

smells, Gidget protested being stuffed into a cardboard box with air holes in it. "Meoowww!"

"Hey, no scratching," the boy said. "I wish I could keep you. What would we name you?"

"My name is Gidget." She scratched him again.

The boy set a handful of dry cat food next to her. She didn't eat it.

"You're not keeping that nasty kitten," The Mom said. "We've got enough cats around here. I can smell them all around the garden. Now that it's a bit cooler, I gotta spray for nematodes before they get to the zucchini roots."

She took Gidget to the shelter the next day.

 "That's what everybody does," Gidget said.

"What?" Clawed asked.

"Spray bug poison on their gardens and lawns, the trees and flowers too."

"Sage and Ben do too. So?"

"Sage and Ben don't use poison. The stuff they use is organic. You do know what organic is, don't you?"

Clawed ignored her. If Gidget wanted to believe he was a dumb couch potato, so be it.

Gidget went on. "Chemical fertilizers and pesticides make

all the animals sick too. When it rains, it leaches down the hill and runs off to the drainage ditches…"

"Take it easy. You're going to have a heart attack."

"Seriously, Clawed, they think they're growing a garden. But they're killing the rivers, and the fish. And the land! And that's only part of the problem."

Clawed yawned. "There's more?"

"Junk."

"Junk?"

"That's what I said. Do you know how much of the earth is wasted when people throw away stuff like mattresses, dog toys, refrigerator magnets, rings, and other shiny things— bling."

"Did you say 'bling'?"

"Yeah, so?"

"That's what the garden beyond the rose arbor is called."

Gidget's ears perked forward. "That explains it."

"Explains what?"

"What's wrong with the garden. The Blinglings are more worried about worthless treasures than the plants they're supposed to take care of."

"Hmm." Clawed couldn't sleep now. "What happened after you went to the shelter?"

Chapter 16

The day dawned bright and clear

perfect for a day at the fair. A touch of humidity moistened the morning breeze. Monarchs competed for juicy milkweed blossoms. All around the garden, the Blinglings were waking up.

Piggy Pomp yawned and stretched. Lying on her back, she tossed from left to right, scratch, scratch, scratch. Remembering it was Fair Day, she rolled over and stood. "Snort, oink, what a beautiful day."

Joey nudged Stevie. "Get up!"

"Yawwwnnnn…"

"It's Fair Day."

Stevie rubbed his little pink nose. "Huh?" He yawned again, opened one eye, and looked at his brother. "Oh yeah!" Then, Stevie was up too.

Andy-Bob a green parrot flew overhead. "It's Fair Day! It's Fair Day. Get up, get up. It's Fair Day. Who is, who is, who is going to win today?"

Fire-orange honeysuckle flowers waved good morning to the sun. Rising above the delicate sensitive vine, violet powder-puff blooms bobbled in the breeze. A weathered St. Francis statue stood as still as an English guard protecting the garden.

Sage was already out weeding. "No grass allowed." She pulled at the ever-reaching root runner that tied all the green blades together in a foothold where Sage didn't want it. "You don't belong here." She sat back on her heels and inhaled the fragrant air. "Ahh, I love morning. Hi, Clawed."

"Hi Sage." He quickly stifled a meow that sounded more like a baby's whine. "Can I pleeeeease come out?" He patted the screen.

"Don't do that, Clawed. You have to understand. You're inside for your own good."

"Hmph; good, shmood." He hung his head over the edge of his platform.

Sage inspected the rose arbor. Here and there, new leaves had already withered. A few gangly branches held fully grown leaves and a bud or two, an open bloom here and there, but not the usual abundance of blooms.

Moving away from the arbor, she carefully plucked curled passion-vine tendrils from their grasp in the screen and moved them onto the trellis where a scraggly growth of foliage fed a host of Gulf fritillary caterpillars.

Some looked like they were standing on the ends of their wriggly bodies and waving. Others were morphing into a chrysalis. Exposed to the outside elements, their caterpillar skin hardened to a form that resembled a dried leaf, excellent camouflage while in a state of change.

Still inspecting the rose bush, Sage gazed into a drop of water nestled in the crook between two leaves. Prismatic light reflected off its shimmering surface. As a soft breeze tousled the leaves, the tiny globule of water shifted, took shape, then slid down the stem of the plant and disappeared.

Sage blinked and shook her head. "It can't be," she said. "Water drops aren't supposed to look like pigs."

Maybe Sage, like Tabbert, could see them, too. "They are if you're a Blingling," Clawed said.

He wished she understood him. He wished *he* understood him. Hmm. He wondered for the umpteenth time where Tabbert was.

Piggy Pomp left her resting place and headed to the pond. She peered at her reflection in its surface. "I hope I win today."

Categories in the competition for a lottery ticket were: Most Beautiful, Best Muscles, Shiniest, Tallest, Plumpest, and more. But not everyone could win. Some would have to wait until next year for a chance.

No one had ever seen what this treasure looked like. Piggy Pomp imagined a soft pillow, round and pearly pink, and as huge as her rump. To the monarchs, it was a purple diamond set in the middle of the butterfly pool where they could rest and sip from the water without getting their feet wet. To Joey and Stevie, it was a piece of cheese so large they'd never have to search for food again.

Caught up in the excitement, Lil tried to picture the one thing that would take away all her responsibilities and fill her with a sense of peace. Another cat maybe?

By ones, two by two, and threes, the Blinglings headed toward the fairground. They slid down leafy stems and glided across pebbles to the clearing where moss-covered rocks made for great seating in the shade of the crocodile ferns. What a great day.

Two turtles, Curly and Larry, plodded along.

"We're going to the fa–air. We're going to the fa-air," Larry said.

"It's going to be a hot one," Curly said. "I'm glad the fair is by the pond."

Larry nodded. "Mm hmm."

 Deep in the underwater cavern, Tabbert sat back.

"That voice says I'm going to move this treasure piece thing." He listened for the voice to tell him how. At first, he didn't hear anything. Then, ding-clang-pings tinkled softly over his head.

He looked up. The bright light beaming down onto the treasure chest had dimmed. Oblong shadows circled in the watery space above the clear dome that encapsulated the cavern.

He gazed into the monstrous treasure piece glowing before him. More than half his size, it was so clear he could almost see through it. He stared into it for a long time.

"I'm going to get you out of here," Tabbert stared into the jewel, "even if I break my back doing it."

The deeper he looked into the facets, the more fractured his image became, until all he could see were many reflections of his own face.

The wind chimes ding-clanged more distinctly.

"I heard that." He cocked his head. "I know I heard that." His tail switched back and forth. His tongue flicked in and out. His eyes rotated around and around searching for a way out. He looked up again. The shadowy forms above swam faster. Something was happening.

"I know you're coming," Lil said. She wasn't entirely sure Stocker was going to the fair, but she did believe that he should, especially since she didn't have a clue about what was going to happen today.

Stocker looked through the undergrowth toward the clearing where the Blinglings were gathering.

"Shep and I will be leaving shortly," Lil said. "He has to select the Picker."

Stocker nodded slightly, but still did not reply.

"Any ideas?"

Stocker shook his head.

Lil sighed."Half the time, I don't know what I'm doing. I wish you'd say something."

"You lead the Blinglings, Lil. You encourage them and ground them, Lil. The treasure has mesmerized them. They need you."

"Does this really have to happen?"

"Yes, and it's your job to guide them through it. You say things in a much better way than I do. If I were to tell them that life as they know it will change today, it would scare them. It would ruin the fair, Lil. You've tried long enough to warn them. Now, they must be shown." His voice trailed off, and he didn't speak again.

Lil sighed. Even though it seemed that Stocker was being straight with her, she still didn't know what was going to happen. How was life as *she* knew it going to change? Sometimes relying on faith was the most difficult thing to do. She headed out to find Shep.

They walked side by side, Shep listening with patient calm, Lil spitting with frustration. She had never admitted to anyone that she couldn't remember what had come before, but now she admitted it to Shep.

"Why can't I remember?"

"Why are you still going on about that?"

Lil stopped on the trail and looked at her friend. "You're wondering too, I know you are."

Shep stared at his feet. "Trust," he said. "Just, trust."

They continued walking, neither looking right nor left. Shuffling along, they focused on one thing. A winner.

It was going to be a long day.

Chapter 17

Wind chimes rang

the judges were coming. Piggy Pomp scraped her back once more on the rough bark of the bougainvillea trunk. She scratched and rubbed until her piggy skin glowed.

Joey and Stevie groomed each other. Stevie accidentally nipped Joey's ear.

He yelped. "Ouch! You did that on purpose."

"SorrEEEE! I did not!" Stevie perked an ear to the sky. "Hear that? Hurry, we're almost at the fairgrounds."

The frogs Romeo and Juliet hopped faster, their frumpy forms springing into the air then plopping down again. Curly and Larry steadily plodded on.

All jostled for space and searched for familiar faces. There was Bella the pink bunny and, "Oh, hey," there was Teddy

Bear. Towering above everyone, Necky the giraffe scanned the growing crowd.

Piggy Pomp stood next to Necky. "Cool! Wow! They're coming from everywhere." She squealed. "I'm so excited"

Tik, Tak, and Tuk, the penguins crackled as a happy hum mounted in the air. Mice, turtles, frogs, rabbits, and roosters, all iridescent and crystal-clear as the purest water, filled the clearing.

A  pair of monarchs sat side by side, their wings folded. More fluttered by. "Looks like fun, huh?"

"Mm hmm, sure does. A little windy today."

"Good flying weather."

The chimes rang again, and the crowd quieted. Lil and Shep slid up onto a flat rock.

Piggy Pomp squealed. "There they are."

"That's weird," Necky said. They don't look very happy."

"Hush," Piggy said. "They're officials; they're supposed to be serious."

"Lil isn't like that. She's friendly, and she's even funny sometimes."

Piggy Pomp snorted. "I mean, today is Fair Day! They're the judges. I'm glad I'm not a judge."

"Me too."

Lil meowed and raised a paw. "All right everyone." The hubbub turned to a whisper.

"Thank you all for coming. Today, the best of the best will be rewarded. You've all worked hard in order to be ready for this moment."

"What a bunch of hooey," Stevie whispered.

"What do you mean by that?" Joey asked.

"Lil doesn't even believe in this. Why is she acting like she does. This isn't all that it's cracked up to be. Something else is going on."

"You don't know that."

"That's right, I don't know."

"Why doubt? Why not believe? Just think, you could win the prize for being the Smallest Bully."

Stevie nipped Joey's ear. "That *was* on purpose."

Lil continued. "At the end of the day, someone will leave with a treasure, but right now, let's get down to business and find out who our finalists are. Contestants have five minutes to gather in a circle." She and Shep stepped off the platform.

The wind chimes sang again.

Twenty minutes later, some contestants became restless and stepped out of their poses. Others complained to those standing nearby.

"What are we waiting for?" Piggy asked.

"Is everybody here?" Towering over everyone's heads, Necky looked out over the crowd. "Isn't Tabbert coming? It is his birthday, after all."

"But, he's not really a Blingling," Piggy said. "He can go in and out. We can't."

"So, he may be different, but that doesn't mean he's not one of us."

Piggy snorted and turned her back on Necky.

The frogs croaked softly. "What are we waiting for?"

"Gak, gak, gak." The penguins nodded and flapped their stubby wings.

"Ring-cling-a-ling-ding," sang the wind chime. Everyone held their breath.

Shep's slow, steady voice brought them to attention. "It's time to announce the finalists."

The contestants huffed and preened, puffed and flexed, licked their lips, and batted their eyes.

"The winner for the Most Perseverant... is a tie. Two tickets will be given for this prize."

The contestant's eyes sparkled.

"The winners are Turtles, Curly and Larry. You two pressed on today even with all the scuffling, flitting, and running about going on. You have trained well." Shep handed each a ticket.

Romeo won the Ploppingest Hopper. Everyone nodded. He was definitely rounder since he and Juliet had gotten together. When thrusting himself three feet or more, a most excellent hop, he would land on his belly with a resounding PLOP.

Necky won for the Tallest. Of course. The lottery ticket he held in his teeth fluttered in the breeze.

There seemed to be a category for everything, making it easy to forget that only so many could win a ticket. The growing excitement was electric.

"The winner of the Most Hurrisome is—" It was so quiet you could have heard a pine needle drop, "Tabbert!"

Nodding, everyone took a deep breath.

"So right!" Stevie said. "He is the Most Hurrisome."

"Where is he?" Necky asked looking around. The crowd shifted and shuffled. "Who will hold his ticket?"

Joey called. "Tabbert! Yo...ho.... Tabbert?"

'Ding, cling.'

Trapped in the pond's watery depths, Tabbert heard the "ding, clang."

"I hear you; I hear you." He spun in a circle. His eyes rolled 180 degrees in their sockets. He had to get out of here. He wrapped his front legs around the jewel and strained to lift it. His body turned the same color as the gem. Gold and crimson waves surged through him.

Steadfast and motionless, the Dilitz maids stared intently at the treasure chest.

Shep went on. "And now... the Most Beautiful"

The fact that Tabbert had not stepped forward to claim his ticket was quickly forgotten.

Once again, the crowd straightened their shoulders, took deep breaths, and turned right and left in the sun. Their shining facets became a blur of rainbow-colored beams.

Squirming with anticipation, Piggy whispered. "Pick me, pick me." She looked at the Blingling standing closest to her; Bella, a bunny with pretty ears and glittering eyes. A pang of jealousy tore at Piggy's gut.

"The winner is…PIGGY POMP!"

Piggy squealed and whirled —almost trampling Juliet, the Most Adoring, who hopped out of the way at the last second. Everyone clapped and cheered and bumped shoulders in satisfied camaraderie.

Piggy glanced at Bella. Tears glistened in her eyes. How beautiful the little rabbit truly was.

Tabbert strained with all his might, but still could not move the gem. Light beams from the jewel sparkled in his eyes.

"Shep will now tell us who he has chosen to be the Picker." Stocker announced.

How would Shep choose?

Lil didn't move. All eyes turned to Shep. Everyone held their breath. Even the fragrant breeze stopped blowing. No bees hummed. No wing flitted. No caterpillar munched.

"Wait," Piggy said. "Can Bella hold Tabbert's ticket?"

All eyes turned to the flop-eared bunny who hadn't won anything. "Would you mind, Bella?" Shep asked.

"I'd be glad to." Bella slid up to the rock, retrieved Tabbert's ticket, and then slid back to her place in the crowd.

Piggy Pomp slipped a foreleg around Bella's shoulders. "If I win the treasure, I'll share it with you."

"Aww, thanks Piggy. You don't have to do that."

"Of course, I do." They looked back at Shep.

"All right then," he said. "Since he has chosen not to participate in the competitions, it seems only fair that I have chosen Lay-Z to pick the winning ticket. Someone find him, please. We can't proceed without him."

Everyone searched the crowd for Lay-Z's telltale hump.

Zodiaq the rooster found him napping under the plumbago bush and had to peck him on the head to wake him.

"Everything seems fair so far," Joey said to his brother. "What do you have to say about all this now?"

"I don't know." Stevie called out. "Hold on a sec. How is Lay-Z going to choose? What if he has favorites?"

Shep hadn't thought of that. Even the wisest of the wise don't know everything. He answered quickly. "He will choose blindfolded."

Stevie frowned and scratched his ear. That didn't make sense, but he didn't have a better idea.

"Okay now, everyone with a ticket, stand over there by the shore.

Piggy Pomp and Bella held hands. Stevie and Joey high-fived. Curly and Larry thumped shells.

*

Inside his crystal cavern, Tabbert's eyes were drawn deeper into the colors swirling inside the gem.

*

The butterflies draped a blindfold made of elephant ear leaves over Lay-Z's eyes.

"Wait. Why me? I didn't choose to be any part of this."

Shep gently nudged Lay-Z's leg. "And that's exactly why I chose you, Lay-Z. You'll do fine."

"I didn't get my bearings before you blindfolded me."

"Don't overthink it. You've got this." Shep spun the camel around three times, and three times again, then stopped spinning him. "Now, pick someone."

"I'm dizzy." Lay-Z said. "You have to help me."

"You're on your own," Shep said then turned to the crowd. "Spread out everyone."

Lay-Z took a deep breath and shook his head. "Should I tap someone on the head? Where is everybody?" He raised his head and turned it from side to side. His nostrils flared; his ears perked up.

"He can't tap someone on the head." Stevie whispered into Joey's ear. "That's not fair. Necky is taller than he is, and we're way down here. We don't stand a chance."

"Will you be quiet." Joey nipped Stevie's rump.

Stevie squeaked. "Who's the Smallest Bully now."

Lil's voice rose above the murmuring crowd. "Remember Lay-Z. You can only pick one, so take your time."

How would he do it? Was he partial to Piggy's smell? Would he shy away from Romeo's froggy aroma? Doubtful glances passed from one to another.

Stocker stepped into the clearing. No one noticed. All eyes were glued on Lay-Z.

The wind chime sang. "Ring…a…ting…ding-a-ling…ling…ling," and stopped.

*

Tabbert clung to the gem, his rotating eyes following lightning rays flashing within it. He became the jewel, cold, hard. And yet somehow, he could still feel his heart beating; with every pulse, the colors swirled within the stone like it was sucking the life force from him. And, now he couldn't let it go.

*.

 Tortured with indecision, Lay-Z shifted his weight from one foot to the other and swung his head from side to side. Right here. What to do? Right now. He didn't like being put on the spot. Stocker would know what to do. Stocker knew everything. But Stocker hardly ever talked to anyone besides Lil. She had come with Shep, and Shep had said Lay-Z was on his own.

"Oh golly," Lay-Z said. "I'm just going to do this." He plunged his head down, down, down. Water filled his nostrils and his ears. He shook his head. The blindfold washed away from his eyes. He opened them. Everything became clear to him then.

"Whoah!" Water gushed down from the domed ceiling. It rose around Tabbert's ankles, then covered his belly, climbed up his back, and had about reached his nostrils when…

Lay-Z wrapped his tongue around Tabbert and the treasure piece.

"What! Arrrrggggghh! Put me down."

"Shorry Tabbert, hanngonn." Lay-Z mumbled through his mouthful. He raised his head out of the water and flung the jewel with Tabbert clinging to it over the Blinglings' heads to the edge of the clearing where it dropped onto the ground.

"Oh my," Piggy said.

Bella clapped. "Beautiful!"

Stevie hmphed. "See I told you this was a bunch of hooey. He isn't even a Blingling."

Tabbert tumbled and somersaulted across the grass. "Ooof!" He lost his breath for a second, but was instantly on his feet and found himself standing in front of Stocker.

"Happy Birthday, Tabbert," Stocker said. "Glad you could join us. You've been picked. How do you like your prize?"

Chapter 18

Life at the shelter

was mind-boggling. Gidget wasn't sure she liked it. She had never seen so many cats in one place, not even in Farmer Hudson's barn. An old residence converted into a cat shelter housed at least one hundred felines ranging in age from newborn to ancient. The place stank so badly her eyes burned.

"My boy found her in the orchard," the boy's mom said to the woman who ran the shelter. "I'd keep her, but we've got so many already."

When the woman opened the box, Gidget dashed into the kitchen, ran into an open, base cabinet, and huddled in its darkest corner.

Later, when the woman reached in to get her out, Gidget hissed and raked razor-sharp claws across the woman's arm.

"Ouch! You're a scrapper, aren't you?" The woman moved away. "Okay, if that's the way you want it, I'll leave you alone. I guess you'll come out when you're hungry."

For the next month, Gidget ate and slept in that kitchen cabinet and slipped out only long enough to use a litter box. She developed the habit of carrying around a catnip-stuffed mouse in her mouth. It gave her comfort. She often cried into the soft cloth, swallowing tears that came out of nowhere. She had lost mother and now, her only friends. What had become of sweet Daisy, and the curly-haired girl? She'd even be happy if she could see that annoying Tikky.

Fighting off other challenging cats, Gidget adopted the hidden recess of the wooden cabinet as her own. Maybe she'd stay in there forever.

It was not to be so. The first time a family adopted Gidget, she ran through their home looking for a place to hide.

She cowered under a bed and scratched anyone who attempted to pull her out. When the family brought her back to the shelter, she ran to her cabinet, displaced a younger feline, and settled back into the familiar routine of shelter life.

An old man who adopted her had no problem with her staying in the cabinet under the bathroom sink. "That's right

126

where the mice come through," he said.

She sniffed the ragged hole around the drain pipe, but nothing ever came out of it. A mouse wouldn't have lasted a minute if there'd been one.

Over time, the gray and brown stripes on her face and the pea-sized brown spots on her belly deepened to a warm luster. She'd had respiratory issues ever since she'd almost drowned in Farmer Hudson's cow pond, and everything made her sneeze. She slept in a pile of musty rags, constantly breathed through swollen nostrils, and her eyes watered all the time.

She learned to squat over the commode for her toileting needs and washed regularly despite the poor living conditions.

The man only fed her once a day and very little at that. Gidget was used to being hungry. At least she didn't have to guard her food from a bunch of feline thieves.

The safety of the day-to-day monotony ended sooner than she hoped.

One day, the man grabbed her out of the dark recess of the bathroom vanity. "Gotta let you go, girlie. I'm moving and can't take you with me." The man stuffed her in a box and closed the lid.

Gidget did her best to keep from rolling around, but the box in motion pitched her from one corner into another until movement came to an abrupt halt. Thunk!

An engine coughed and came to life. Vibrations tickled the bottoms of her feet, and a sudden lurch sent her rolling into another corner.

She didn't know how long she sat that way before the humming pulsations of the engine stopped. Her ears pricked up at the click of a door opening, the thump of footsteps, another door opening. Her muscles tightened as the box, seeming to move with a life of its own, pitched and tossed her about.

Inside, Gidget was suddenly airborne for a few seconds before the box hit something solid, tumbled and rolled, then fell open. Bright sunlight pierced her eyes. She was on the ground.

"Git going, kitty." A large, booted foot gave her a not-so-gentle nudge. She ran across a short span of grass, dashed under a nearby tangle of brush, and didn't move.

The man got back in the car, slammed the door, and left. She listened until she could no longer hear the car, and still, she didn't move.

Eventually, shadows devoured the daylight. She slept in fits, her legs twitching as she dreamed of running inches ahead of an avalanche of soggy earth tumbling around her. Shiny creatures caught in the tumult, mud, and rocks sucked at her heels. Rain, torrential rain, she was swimming, so tired, barely able to breathe. That part always woke her.

Hunger drove her out of hiding. Crouching low to the ground, she crept deeper into the woods. Rustling in the leaves stopped her. Two tiny eyes blinked. Gidget sprang and captured the unsuspecting mole in her sharp claws. Supper.

She washed her face, then continued a cautious inspection of the woods and came upon a clearing. She recognized the grocery cart. It still had the cardboard in the bottom of it. Tikky and Daisy were nowhere to be found. She meowed softly.

As a gentle rain fell, she rolled into a tight ball on the damp ground under the cart and listened to night peepers and the hoots of a great horned owl.

She didn't miss the clutter of cats at the shelter, but a dull ache constantly gnawed at the pit of her stomach; eating the mole hadn't made it go away. Finally drifting off to sleep...

"Hey there, little sister. Whatcha doing?"

Gidget woke immediately. Prepared to run or fight, she dug her claws into the moist ground and hissed.

"Hey, I know you, don't I?"

Gidget spun around and found herself staring into the face of an orange cat twice her size. She sniffed and immediately recognized him. "Tikky?"

"In the fur." He sat back and smiled. "Never thought I'd see you again."

Gidget stared.

"Still as talkative as ever, I see." Tikky hunkered up next to her. "Mind if I share your shelter?"

Gidget flinched but didn't move. "Where's Daisy?" she asked.

"I don't know. The day you didn't come back, I stayed up in the tree for the longest time. Didn't come down until the next day. She wasn't in the cart anymore. I figured she climbed out and left. Like you."

"Like you and me, you mean. I planned on going back until one of those boys took me. You look well fed."

"Mm, hm." Tikky yawned. "I'm tired."

His closeness gave Gidget comfort. Within minutes, a duet of quiet purring joined the other songs of the night.

The rain tapered off. With the warmth of a friend nearby, Gidget slept soundly.

A human voice startled her awake in the morning. She fled to the cover of the underbrush.

"Aww, kitties!"

That voice sounded familiar. Gidget wasn't sure, so she stayed hidden.

Tikky strutted out into broad daylight.

"Hi, Tikky." The curly-haired girl petted him. "Where'd you find Gidget, huh? That is her, isn't it? Come here, Gidget; here kitty, kitty."

Gidget peered through the thick foliage.

Rattle, rattle.

Gidget knew that sound, but didn't budge.

Meg wiped out a dish, filled it with crunchies, and set it on the ground. "Tikky, don't eat it all. Come on out, Gidget. Where are you?"

While Tikky gobbled the food, Meg pushed aside wet branches and peered beneath tangled bushes. "Gidget. Come out. I'm not going to hurt you."

Gidget didn't move, even when Meg almost stepped on her. Brown and gray striped fur was the perfect camouflage.

Meg put a dry piece of cardboard onto the bottom of the crate and poured another dishful. After playing with them for a while, she left. "I'll be back tomorrow. Tikky, leave some of that for Gidget."

Tikky had eaten all the food by the time Gidget came out of hiding.

"Are you a cat or a pig?"

"Aren't we sassy?" Tikky said.

He could have left her some, but what good would arguing with him do?

She'd show him. They might hunt together and keep each other warm, but next time she found food, she wasn't sharing...period. Obviously, Tikky could fend for himself. He'd survived this long in the wilderness.

Could she?

Chapter 19

Gidget spent a lot of time with Tikky

but didn't come out of hiding when the curly-haired girl was around.

Gidget wasn't in the mood for more of people's dusty cabinets or lurching boxes. She'd gotten used to fending for herself. Bird feathers and lizard tails littered the clearing.

"Hey, I've got something fun to do today," Tikky said.

"What?"

"Let's see how the new house is coming along."

Gidget hesitated. "I don't know."

"Nobody's there today. Come on. It'll be fun."

Gidget didn't like going to the construction site. The noisy equipment made her fur stand on end, and vibrations from the motors prickled the bottoms of her feet.

"The last time we went there, workers threw rocks at us."
She hadn't talked to Tikky for days after that.

"Yeah, and remember I found that leftover roast beef sandwich?"

Hungry, she reluctantly agreed to follow him.

On their way, Tikky stopped to check out Sage and Ben's yard. "Sometimes the lady who lives here leaves treats out," Tikky said. "I don't see any today. Oh yeah, a black cat lives there, too. Dummy tried to mess with me one day. I showed him who was boss; bit his foot when he took a swipe at me."

"Uh huh." It hadn't quite happened that way. She'd seen the fight, but she didn't tell him.

Tikky dashed across the yard. "Come on."

They approached the construction site.

No one was around. Gidget walked across the dry, fluffy sand surrounding the house. Her nostrils flared. She took a shallow breath. No dust. So far, so good.

Tikky ran up the driveway, past a stack of roof trusses, into the open structure, and disappeared.

Gidget looked back over her shoulder. Everything seemed fine. Even the huge machine that pounded a very long pipe into the ground was quiet. Tikky called it a well digger. The whole ground shook when it was working. Sometimes at night, she could still hear it banging in her ears.

She found Tikky with his head buried in a white paper bag. Ketchup and mustard clung to his whiskers.

He burped. "Yum, cheeseburger."

"Did you save me any?"

Looking a bit sheepish, Tikky turned back to the bag.

"Thanks a lot." Gidget said.

"Next one is yours. Promise."

Gidget climbed over piles of boards, tiptoed around rolls of wire, and leaped over pipes. Used to the cushioning of the woodsy, pine-needled ground, the hard, concrete floor irritated her feet.

Tikky called from a dark corner. "Here! I found this for you."

Gidget sniffed the crust of bread and the white gooey substance slathered on it, then looked at Tikky. Crumbs clung to his whiskers, and he was still licking his chops.

"You're hopeless," she said.

"I saved you some, didn't I?"

She didn't eat it. "I'm leaving."

"We just got here."

"And, you can stay if you want. This place gives me the creeps." She couldn't explain why the construction site made her throat feel like it was being sucked into her stomach. Kind of like the sickening weightlessness she'd felt when the old man had tossed the box, with her in it, into the bushes.

A sudden chill ran down her spine.

When Gidget and Tikky returned to the shopping cart in the woods, they found smoke rising from the fire pit and a tent pitched close by.

"Someone's here. Maybe the girl brought us something," Tikky said.

A group of boys came into the clearing. Gidget fled to the cover of a nearby bush. She remained hidden there while the boys cooking something that smelled delicious on sticks over the fire. She wished she'd eaten that nasty leftover sandwich Tikky had found. Settling for a mole and a palmetto bug, she fell into a fitful sleep.

She dreamed of the pounding of the well digger, of running, running, running, of falling to the bottom of a huge hole, and water everywhere. She struggled to climb out of the hole, but the deluge of water kept washing her back into it.

In the morning, the pounding of the digging machine woke her. She peered through the bushes.

136

Meg was holding a bag and was talking to the boys. "Did you guys see two cats last night? A fluffy orange one and a skinny, grayish-brown tabby?"

"Not recently." One boy told her how he and his friends had found two kittens. They'd rescued one. The other had climbed a tree.

"What happened to the one you rescued?"

"My mom wouldn't let me keep it. She took it to the shelter the next day. That was a couple of months ago."

"I don't know how, but she ended up back here. At least, I think it's her," Meg said. "If you see them again, will you please leave them alone? I'm trying to find homes for them."

"Yeah, sure."

"And before you leave, would you put this food in that dish?"

"Yup, okay."

Gidget and Tikky stayed hidden for most of the day. When the boys packed up and departed, Tikky ran straight to the food dish. Gidget ran beside him, only a whisker away. She wasn't about to miss another meal.

Tikky gobbled so much of the food she was lucky to get some.

Then he ran off. He was gone a long time.

By the end of the second day, she was tired of eating moles and bugs, which was why she came out of hiding when Meg came along rattling a box crunchies.

"Gidget," Meg whispered. She knelt slowly and offered the bowl of food.

Gidget crept across the clearing, stopping often, her eyes darting around the open space, alert for the least hint of danger. She dipped her head into the food.

She'd taken only a few bites before she was snatched by the scruff of her neck. She couldn't move, felt paralyzed, much the same as when Mother had carried her as an infant.

"I'm sorry Gidget. We're going on vacation and I don't want you to be alone. Anyways, it's time you had a good home."

Meg wrapped Gidget in a soft blanket. No matter how loud Gidget yowled or how much she tore at the fabric, she could not get free.

"It's going to be all right, Gidget. I promise."

Gidget burrowed into the sweater as Meg, carrying her, left the woods.

After some time, Meg stopped. Gidget peeked out of the confining wrap and found herself facing a door. Meg knocked on it.

Sage opened the door. "Hi there, Meg."

"Hi, Mrs. Foley. Um…"

"What do you have there?"

"I found this kitten in the woods. My dad won't let me keep it. I've been taking care of her. I named her Gidget." Words continued to gush out of Meg's mouth. "When I first found her, there were three of them."

"Three?"

"Uh huh. The calico has been gone for a while, but there's a fluffy, orange one out there, too. That's Tikky. He's hard to catch." She looked down at Gidget. "Well…so was she."

"Yes, I've seen the orange one around. You've been feeding them?"

"Yes. But we're going away for a whole month, and I'm worried. She's so little and a bit of a scaredy cat. Not like Tikky. He's not scared of anything. I'm afraid Gidget won't get enough food while I'm gone, and I was wondering…" Meg paused and looked down at the bundle she held in her arms. "Would you take her, Mrs. Foley?"

Sage reached for the bundle in Meg's arms. "Let me hold her a minute."

"I've been trying to catch her for a month. I was lucky to catch her today." She handed Gidget to Sage. "Usually, Tikky comes running right out to me, but I haven't seen him for a couple of days."

"Oh, I wouldn't worry too much about him," Sage said. "We feed him, too. Come in. Let's see if we can get her out of the sweater. Close the door tight."

"Hi, Mr. Foley."

"Hi, Meg. What do you have there?"

Sage answered for her. "A stray kitten."

"Oh?" Ben raised an eyebrow. "Company for Clawed?"

Clawed had been watching the whole thing from his spot on the back of the couch. Interesting. Very interesting.

Chapter 20

While Meg repeated the story

about finding Gidget in the woods, Ben helped Sage retrieve the tense ball of fur from the yellow sweater.

Exposed and vulnerable, Gidget hissed.

Ben drew her close to his chest. "Shush, little kitty. It's okay." He looked at Meg who looked back at him with pleading eyes. "Her heart's beating a hundred miles a minute. Can't you bring her home?"

Silly question. Hadn't Ben heard her say that she was going on vacation?

"No, Dad says we have enough strays already."

Sage patted Gidget's head.

Gidget buried her face in Ben's armpit. "Go get Clawed," he said.

Here goes, Clawed thought.

Sage picked him up. She held him firmly under one arm and clasped his two front feet with her other hand. Now what did she have to do that for? It wasn't like he wanted to get away.

He definitely wanted to see this little stranger. He could smell her intensity from five feet away.

She was kind of cute even though she was still hissing. Ben held her up to him.

Gidget hissed and swiped at Clawed's face, but Ben pulled her away.

"Relax, girl," Clawed said. "Nobody's going to hurt you." Trying to be friendly, he stretched out to let her sniff him.

Gidget hissed again. Clawed backed off. "Okay, have it your way. You'll figure it out sooner or later."

"Good boy, Clawed." Sage patted his head and smiled at Ben. "What do you think, hon?"

"Do I have a choice?" He smoothed Gidget's fur, and even though she hissed again, this time she seemed less intense.

Sage set Clawed back on the couch. "It looks like your little Gidget has a new home. Come over and see her when you get back."

"I will." Meg jumped up and down and clapped her hands. "Thank you so much."

After Meg left, Sage locked the front door and closed all the bedroom doors. When Ben set Gidget down, she bolted across the tile floor, her feet getting no purchase on the slick, hard surface. She scampered into the living room, crouched down on the area rug, dug her claws into the pile, and yowled.

What a nervous Nellie.

Gidget settled under the dining room table. Sage placed a blanket by her and a dish of food next to it.

"Don't eat it, Clawed."

As if. He wasn't going anywhere near that hissing demon until she settled down.

The food was gone in the morning. Sage refilled it. "I hope you didn't eat that, Clawed."

"I didn't," Clawed meowed. He ate his own breakfast, slipped out the cat door, climbed to the top of his tower, and ignored everybody for the better part of the morning.

He didn't stay angry for long. He went back in and sat a short distance away from Gidget. "I see you ate, and you also figured out that the litter box is on the back deck. Glad to know you're not glued to that spot under the table. You ever going to come out from under there in broad daylight?"

Gidget hissed.

By the end of her first week, Gidget was skirting the living area of her new surroundings. It would take her a while before she trusted this new situation—or anything, or anyone.

She roamed the house at night, inspecting every corner of the inside and the back porch, and even climbed up to the first platform on Clawed's cat tower at his coaxing. She favored a catnip mouse Sage bought for her and carried it around in her mouth, crying through it half the time.

"What's that about?" Clawed asked her one day.

She mumbled through the mouse. "None of your business."

Sitting up on the top platform, Clawed thought about Dr. Phil. On one of his TV shows, he'd said, "Sometimes longings for old friends and the quiet safety of comfortable places we knew so well, rise up so strongly in us that we can't help but cry."

That was probably what was wrong. She was missing wherever she had come from. The first chance Gidget got, would she run away? To where?

When Ben cut the hole in the screen, she found out she didn't really want to run away anymore.

144

When she became more comfortable talking to Clawed, she told him. "The first time I jumped out, I ran back into the woods to look for Tikky, but I couldn't find him."

Maybe living in the woods wasn't such a good idea after all, she'd said. They were all gone. First her mother, then Daisy, and then Tikky. "Were you listening the day Ben read a newspaper article to Sage about the coyotes?"

A family of hungry coyotes wouldn't hesitate to eat a cat if they came upon one.

That Gidget, she was a smart one. Clawed had no doubt that she knew a lot more about what was going on with that horrid gem than she was saying. He'd have to figure out a way to get her to tell him. Or wait. Darn it. Patience. Hmph.

Chapter 21

It figured that Tikky

had eaten all the food. "I knew he was a rascal." More unkind names came to mind, but Clawed thought it best not to speak them out loud.

"Oh, really?" Gidget turned her back to him and proceeded to wash her face.

"What's that all about?" Clawed asked.

"Tikky may have liked to eat all the food, but you don't share either."

"You get your own bowl." He waited for her to give him a snarky retort. When she didn't, he pressed the issue. "You didn't expect me to say something nice about him, did you?"

Gidget faced him again. "No, but you have no idea what we've been through."

"Hold on." Clawed raised his paw. "You've barely spoken to me since you came here, and you cry a lot." He shrugged. "I'm just saying."

"I've got plenty of reasons to cry."

"Whatever…"

"Don't whatever me, Mr. Know-it-all. Everything in your world is easy-peasey."

Clawed cut in. "That's not true. I can't go outside. Something is wrong in the garden. My best friend Tabbert is gone for some strange reason; and anyway, when has any of this mattered to you? You've never said you cared."

Fuming, Clawed shook his head. "If I had my way, I'd be outside sharpening my claws on the palm trees right now. Then I'd go to the garden and look around for the Blinglings."

As if she'd read his mind, Gidget said quietly, "I know a way out."

Clawed squinted his eyes. "How?"

"One day, Ben was working in the yard. I was in the litter box out there by patio back door—you know, doing my…er…business?"

Clawed nodded. "Yeah, yeah." TMI.

147

For months she hadn't said a word. Now, she was all kinds of chatty.

He licked a paw then rubbed it across his eye to wipe away a dust pea that had settled on his eyelash. New construction was going on next door. Dust blown into the air by the excavating machinery filtered through the screen.

Gidget sneezed three times before she continued. "Ben tried to come in by the litter box, but the screen door was locked."

"Yeah, so?"

"So—he pulled out a pocket knife and cut a hole in the screen around the door handle. Then, he reached in and unlocked the door from the inside. He came in, straightened the screen, then left."

She hesitated and looked suspiciously over her shoulder, like she was sharing top-secret info or something.

Maybe she was, seeing as how she claimed to know a way out. "Go on," Clawed said.

"Well, he hasn't fixed that hole yet. Want to see?"

"Of course, I want to see." More than that, Clawed wanted OUT.

That afternoon, when Sage and Ben left to go grocery

shopping, they made a beeline out to the back patio.

"Watch this." Gidget climbed onto the ledge, stood on her tip toes, and pulled at the screen. It swayed open.

"I see it!" More than excited, Clawed swiped at her paw as she struggled to loosen her claws from the screen. He stretched over her and poked his head through the hole.

How had he missed this? He climbed over her back and grasped the screen and pulled himself through the hole. The screen gave way with a zipping rip. He landed outside, then shook himself to straighten his ruffled fur.

Wow! He took a deep breath.

"You tore the screen!"

"You can fix that, can't you?" Clawed didn't stick around to watch Gidget pull herself through the hole.

"Hey! Wait for me!" When she caught up, she said, "We'll have to listen for the car so we can go back in when Sage and Ben get home."

Happy to be outside, Clawed ran. Gidget could hardly keep up.

"Oh my gosh," Clawed said when he stopped to catch his breath. "Have you jumped out of that hole before? And, why haven't you told me about it sooner?"

"I don't answer to you. Now, let's go find Tabbert."

149

"I still can't believe you know him."

"I heard him talk about me lots of times."

"You listen in on our conversations? Is there no privacy?"

"You can go back in and pout, Clawedy-kins."

It irked Clawed that Gidget sounded like Tikky.

"I showed you how to get out," she said. "You'd better appreciate it."

He chose not to respond. Nothing could bother him this afternoon. Colorful butterflies flitted over his head. Bees buzzed around the plumbago bush.

He and Gidget explored the shrubs and sunbaked rocks. The rose arbor looked awful. The garden looked droopy. Something was definitely wrong. Or was it only the heat of the afternoon?

Beetles were munching on dried up worms. Caterpillars chewed on leaves covered with a white powdery substance. Must be the salt residue from the artesian-well sprinkler. Sage had told Ben that morning that it seemed like the water was becoming saltier with every passing day.

The TV weatherman was still talking about the drought. So many things Tabbert had told Clawed appeared to be true.

"You're right," Clawed said.

"That's a first," Gidget said. "About what?"

150

"I had no idea about you."

She hissed in his face.

And, here he was trying to be nice. "Why do you have to be so grouchy? I just want to find Tabbert. Let's look over there under the raspberry prickers."

Tabbert wasn't there. And Clawed sure didn't see any shiny, rainbow-colored creatures.

When a car door slammed out front, they high-tailed it back inside. Gidget had barely finished straightening the screen when Sage came in the front door.

"Kitties! We're home."

The night passed slowly. Excited about the next day's explorations, Clawed fell into a fitful sleep.

Over the next few days, when they had occasional opportunities to go out again, Clawed wandered the garden to his heart's content. One afternoon, he rested under a patch of ferns.

"You're in my spot," Gidget said.

"Let's talk about sharing, shall we?"

Gidget growled under her breath, then lay down just inches away. A red-shouldered hawk passed overhead with a mullet caught in its talons.

The beeeeezzzzzing of the cicadas usually calmed him. Today, it grated on Clawed's nerves. "I'm going to look for Tabbert." Gidget didn't follow.

Sniffing his way through the underbrush, Clawed continued his search for Tabbert and some sign of the Blinglings.

As he stepped into the clearing by the stone-lined pond that Ben had built—CLUNK!

"YEOW!" Clawed turned and ran back into the bushes. Something hard had hit him between the eyes. He shook his head. His eyes watered. He blinked a few times to get rid of the stars he was seeing. What in the world?

Gidget was by his side in a cat's breath. "What happened? Are you okay?"

"Something hit me on the head, and I mean hard." Clawed squinted through the brush, then stared at the ground a foot or so in front of him. "What's that?"

It wasn't a rock. It was too perfect and glowing— definitely glowing.

Gidget shook her head and frowned. "It's a gemstone, Mr. You Don't Know-it-all."

Clawed had never seen a gemstone glow like that. Where had it come from? Strange, very strange indeed.

Chapter 22

Tabbert flicked his tail

and spun. When he completed the circle, Stocker was still standing in front of him, his regal rack of horns towering over his sturdy, iridescent body.

"Yes, sir," Tabbert said. "It appears I *have* been picked. Plucked is more like it." He glanced over his shoulder. He was in the clearing not too far from the jewel which was now two times bigger than Tabbert himself! "I'd like to go home now, and I'd like to leave that *thing*…" Tabbert pointed to the jewel, "right there. Please."

Stocker shook his massive head. "Well, Tabbert, it's yours. You've won it."

"No thanks." Tabbert didn't want any part of that thing.

"Then, what shall we do with it?"

"I don't know. Bury it. Throw it back in the pond. I don't care what you do with it, but I don't want it."

"Would you like to give it to someone?"

The Blinglings' eyes glittered and grew larger. They all leaned toward the glowing gemstone.

"No. That thing is evil. Nobody should have it."

"Someone should have it," said Piggy Pomp.

Stevie shook his head. "I don't think so."

Joey bit Stevie's tail. Murmurs and yeses filled the air.

"So be it," Stocker said.

Tabbert blinked, and Stocker was gone, but the gem was still there.

Wanting nothing more than a quiet night on the gutter spout, Tabbert dashed out of the clearing and headed for the rose arbor.

Colorful light beams radiated from the jewel's center. The Blinglings slipped through the grass toward it.

Stocker watched from the crest of the hill behind the garden. "Lil?"

"Yes." She came to his side.

"The jewel has bedazzled them."

"Why?"

"Because they think it has value."

"It is beautiful."

"Has it mesmerized you, too, Lil? Beauty isn't about outward appearances. That's why the flower bed is suffering. The Blinglings are supposed to be custodians of the garden, but they're thinking only of themselves."

"What should I do?"

"Get their attention. Tell them to prepare. A storm is coming."

"What? But…"

"Now," Stocker demanded.

Lil approached the crowd gathering around the glowing jewel. She found Shep. "Stocker told me to tell them that a storm is coming."

"Then do it," he said.

"Why would they care about a storm, and what does it matter anyway? We've been through storms before."

"Stocker said that's what you're supposed to do. That's all you know."

"Yes, Shep. But, what do you think?"

156

"If Stocker says a storm is coming...then, a storm is coming. Go ahead. Tell them, and we'll see what happens next."

Lil worked her way around scattered vines and pine cones to the Blinglings standing closest to the gleaming gem. Was it getting bigger? Up close, it was extremely intimidating.

"My goodness, it's so beautiful," Piggy Pomp squealed. "It's huge. It must be worth ...uhm..."

Joey and Stevie frowned at each other. Necky looked toward the horizon as if the answers were there. The frogs stopped croaking; the penguins stopped dancing.

What *was* it worth?

Lil spoke to the crowd of Blinglings. "It's beautiful," she said.

All nodded in agreement.

"What value does it have when at this moment a storm is coming?" Lil asked.

Cock-a-doodle-doo crowed. "What are you now, a weathercat?" Everyone laughed.

"Stocker told me to tell you to get ready."

The Blinglings'chuckles faded. "For what?" someone asked. The Blinglings stood closer to one another, their facets touching, the whole mass appearing to melt together.

"A storm is coming. Get back to your duties. You must protect the garden."

Dazzling rays drew all eyes away from Lil. The crowd pressed closer to the stone. As its light enveloped the group, their shining iridescence merged with its glowing radiance.

 Clawed was rubbing his forehead.

Tabbert crashed into him.

"Hey, Tabbert. Where have you been? I've been looking all over for you."

Tabbert brushed himself off. "Oh—my—gobwinkies. You won't believe what happened. Wait a sec. You're out. How'd that happen?"

"Gidget happened." They both turned to look at her.

She shrugged.

Clawed asked again. "Where were you?"

"You're not going to believe me. I can hardly believe it myself."

"Try me." Clawed's face smarted where the gemstone had conked him on the head. He licked his paw and swiped it across his injury, then looked at his paw again. No blood. It felt like there should be blood.

Huddling close to Clawed, Tabbert took a deep breath. "Remember the other day I left to find out more about the treasure so I could prove it to you once for all?"

"Yuh," Clawed answered.

"I went to the Blingling pond and called the Dilitz maids. They took me underwater to a cavern where I found a treasure chest. That thing," he pointed to the gem, "jumped out of the treasure chest into my hand and started growing, right before my eyes."

"Jumped?"

Tabbert nodded and crossed his heart. "I swear. Then this booming voice came out of nowhere and told me to take it. I couldn't even lift the stupid thing; I think it's still growing."

Clawed squinted at the gem's brilliance surging throughout the clearing. The bump on his forehead throbbed with every pulse. "I don't like that thing."

"Me neither." Tabbert looked across the clearing at it. "See what it's doing to my friends?"

"Where?" Clawed asked.

Gidget blinked.

"Look at them all." Tabbert gestured toward the Blinglings gathering around the stone.

 "All I see is the jewel," Clawed said.

159

"Hmph," Gidget snuffled and sat back.

"And, I think it *is* growing. What's going on?"

Alarm bells were going off in Clawed's head. His body went rigid. Gidget was standing so close to his side he could feel her whiskers.

"Uhm, I don't know." Tabbert's dewlap flared. "The Blinglings look like they're melting into that thing. I told you it was evil. I've got to warn them."

Clawed couldn't see anything but the weird thing that had conked him on the head, and it was getting bigger by the minute. He looked at Gidget. "Can you see what's happening?"

She'd probably chatted enough for one day, because she didn't answer.

Clawed was certain she knew something. As a matter of fact, it seemed like everybody besides him knew what was going on. "I don't want anything to do with that...that...thing. I'm going inside."

But he didn't. What did Gidget know?

Chapter 23

Enchanted beyond imagination

the Blinglings were losing their angular forms and blending with the radiant jewel. Even Lil and Shep. They were becoming one with the gem. Tabbert ran around them, desperately calling their names. "Piggy! Joey! Come away from there. It's not what you think. Step back before it's too late!"

He grabbed Lil by the ear, but he too was being drawn— no—sucked into the gem's center; he let go and fell backwards, head over tail, away from of the absorbing power of the light.

He glanced back to where he'd left Clawed and Gidget sitting in the brush. His stomach felt hollow. It seemed like it had been days since he'd eaten, but at the moment, he couldn't have swallowed a bug even if it were served to him on a silver leaf.

Tabbert bolted out of the clearing where the Blinglings were gathered around the monstrous gem. He exited Bling through the arbor where, if he had any say in the matter, he'd never go again—except he'd told Clawed he'd be back. He didn't even want to think about that.

He climbed onto his gutter down-spout and stopped to catch his breath, then skittered across the screen, caught a fly, and tried to swallow. It caught in his throat.

He'd been so excited about the fair, and the lottery, and the treasure that he hadn't really stopped to think. All this running back and forth with messages, always messages, blah, blah, blah.

What was so important that he had to be so busy all the time? He couldn't think of a single thing he'd ever said or done that could have prevented what was happening right now.

He envisioned the Blinglings standing around that horrible treasure piece, pressed shoulder to shoulder, and staring at it. He dashed to the ground, snatched up a cricket, and scooted back up the gutter spout with one cricket leg dangling from his mouth. He gulped and sat back. Food didn't make him feel any better.

A stupid bauble. Clearly, it was still growing, and, strangest thing of all, it had sucked the Blinglings into it. No, that couldn't be. He was seeing things. It was hard to figure out what was real.

He'd always been a part of both worlds. That had made him feel very special before. Now, he didn't feel so special.

Stocker had said he had to go back to Bling and help his friends.

Huge problem—Tabbert really didn't want to.

Not with that glowing red stone in there.

Chapter 24

Clawed grew tired of waiting

for Tabbert to return. Accustomed to the lizard running off, Clawed decided it was time to go home. There wasn't anything he could do about that crazy jewel that had practically knocked him out. "I'm going in."

"Forehead still hurt?" Gidget asked.

"I'm fine."

"Well, alrighty then."

Clawed took one last look at the jewel. It seemed to have stopped growing. He slipped through the hole in the screen, then inside the house through the cat door. He passed Sage and

Ben with a quick hello, climbed up onto the back of the couch and stretched out, wondering briefly where Gidget went.

A while later, he woke to the sound of a spoon tapping on his food dish. Suppertime.

"Hey there, big guy." Sage petted him. "What's that bump on your nose? Huh? You and Gidget better not have gotten into a fight."

He meowed and buried his sore nose in the dish.

The evening news was all about the drought. Florida, where the average rain fall was usually upwards of sixty inches a year, was under severe drought warnings. It was supposedly the rainy season, but in the past month there'd been less than an inch of rain. The grass was shriveled and browning. Flowers were sparse, and butterflies were strangely absent.

Sage told Ben. "I tried running the sprinkler this morning, but the pump whined and made such a racket, I turned it off."

"The natural aquifer is low."

"I hope we get that tropical storm the weatherman is talking about."

"We don't need a tropical storm," Ben said. "We need a nice steady rain."

"Yeah, for about a week."

Clawed's ears perked up at the sound of a motor starting up outside.

Sage looked out the window. "I wonder what they're doing over at the construction site."

Ben joined her at the window. "Looks like they're grading the yard. Probably getting ready for sod."

"They shouldn't be putting any sod down. You know they'll fertilize it, then water it every day for the next two weeks even though there's a ban on watering right now. When it does rain, that fertilizer will run off into the drainage ditches, and then get swept into the river.

"Then an algae bloom will suck the oxygen out of the water. That'll kill the fish. The new owners will complain about how bad the river stinks when the fish start to rot, and they'll never admit that their sod has anything to do with it."

Although he agreed, Ben didn't reply. Anything he said would get Sage riled up even more, and he wasn't in the mood for one of her passionate discussions on saving the planet. It had been a long day.

He sat on the couch. "How you doing, Clawed?" He rubbed the bump above Clawed's eyes.

Clawed hissed and dug his claws into the cushion.

Ben looked up at Sage. "Did you see this sore on Clawed's head?"

"I did."

"What do you suppose happened?"

"I don't know."

"Keep an eye on it. Good thing he's not going out these days. It could be worse."

Pretending to be tired, Clawed yawned.

"Where's Gidget?" Ben asked.

"Probably hiding somewhere. Feel like going to the movies?"

"Sure." Ben covered Clawed with the newspaper and turned off the TV. "Pepsi and popcorn for supper. One of my favorites."

After they'd gone, Clawed peered out from under the newspaper tent. He didn't care if it rained. He didn't care about fertilizer runoff. His forehead throbbed. He'd been a whole lot better off when he'd been confined to the house.

Gidget called out to him from under the love seat in the dining room. "I'm sure you'll feel better tomorrow. We have to go back out and see what happened to that jewel."

"Do what you want. I'm not going near that thing."

Chapter 25

Tabbert watched

Clawed and Gidget slip back into the house. He remained hidden behind his gutter spout. Right now, he didn't want to talk to anyone. He didn't really have to go back to Bling, did he?

Messenger? Who'd made him that anyway?

"Tabbert."

The Voice!

Tabbert spun in a circle and bobbed his head. A bright orange flap of skin flared out in an arc below his neck. "What! Where are you? Show yourself."

"Tabbert, go back to Bling. Your friends need you."

"No. I'm not going back. They don't want me. They've got their treasure now. Anyway, that thing sucked them all up. They're gone. Leave me alone. They don't need me."

"You can't really believe that."

"Yes, I do." The voice had a ring of familiarity. Tabbert listened more intently.

As if it had read his mind, the Voice spoke again. "Yes, you know me."

"Stocker?"

"That's what the Blinglings call me."

"You mean that's not your real name?"

"I'm known by many names, Tabbert."

Tabbert shook his head and flared his dewlap again. "Wait a minute. Where are you? What do you want?"

"I want you to go back to Bling and help your friends."

"Why?"

"Because they're lost, Tabbert. They need you."

But the Blinglings had been sucked up into that evil gem. He couldn't help them now. Could he? Tabbert shook his head. "Noooooo...."

No matter what Stocker said, Tabbert wasn't going back to Bling. Nope. Not tonight anyway.

Chapter 26

The next morning

Clawed climbed onto the patio ledge. Outside, clinging to the gutter down-spout, Tabbert gulped down the last of a spider.

"Hey, Tabbert. We waited for you to come back last night. Where were you?"

"Right here." Tabbert frowned.

"What's wrong?"

Tabbert shook his head, but didn't answer.

Clawed pawed the screen. "What's up, Bud?"

When Tabbert didn't reply, Clawed sat back, licked his paw and washed his face. "Ow." The bump on his forehead still hurt like crazy. He looked at his paw. It had something wet on it. He smelled it. Yuck. "Dude! Is there something oozing out of my head?"

The normally chatty lizard didn't answer.

"Tabbert."

"What?"

"Look at my forehead. See if there's something on it, and then tell me what's wrong with you. I've never seen you in such a mood."

Tabbert sighed and peered through the screen. "Why don't you come outside and let me see it?"

"Can't. Sage is home. And anyway, she says I have to go to the vet today. She said it's for my annual check-up, but now I'm thinking it has something to do with this thing on my forehead." He sniffed his paw again.

Tabbert peered closer. "There's a big bump there, and, yeah, there does seem to be something icky in your fur."

"That stone hurt when it hit me."

"No wonder."

"What do you mean?"

"I mean that yesterday, when I left you to go warn my friends that something strange was happening to them...

Clawed interrupted him. "Strange—like what?"

171

"That stone was sucking them up, like water into a sponge…or something." Tabbert's shoulders slumped. His normally bright green coloring paled.

"Really?" Clawed raised his eyebrows, then winced. That hurt, too.

"Really."

"Where are they now?"

"That's just it. I don't know. But the Voice…I mean, Stocker told me last night that I have to go back to Bling and help them."

"The Voice?"

"This is getting so complicated. I don't know what to believe anymore."

"Explain it, slowly."

"What's the use?" Tabbert answered miserably.

"Maybe I can help."

"I doubt it."

"Just tell me."

"Yesterday, did you see anything weird in the clearing?"

"I saw you. I saw that wretched stone. It did seem like it was growing, but I did *not* see the Blingling things. I've never seen them. So, what about the voice."

Tabbert clutched the screen with all four feet. His dewlap flared once. He took a deep breath. "Remember I told you about the voice I heard when I was in the cavern?"

Clawed nodded.

"I heard it again last night. I was here at home when you and Gidget went in. Then, the same voice that I heard when I was in the underwater cave, it talked to me again; only this time, I heard it right here, where I am right now."

"What did it say?"

"It said I have to go back in there and help my friends."

"Did you say that voice is Stocker? He's the main guy of Bling, or something?"

"Yeah—or something."

"Hm, that's interesting." Was Stocker the voice in his own head? Did it talk to everyone? Clawed licked his paw, wiped his sore spot, smelled his paw again, and made a face. "Whew. I think it's infected."

"Yeah," Tabbert said. "Good thing you're going to have it looked at. That stone is the devil itself."

"It's a dumb rock, Tabbert. And when you came flying out of the pond with it, it knocked me on the head. That's all."

"No, that's not all." Tabbert's dewlap flared. "It ate my friends! And I absolutely do not see how going back over there is going to help, AT ALL."

"Tabbert, you're not really going to know that until you *do* go back over there."

"It almost ate *me*."

Clawed scratched his chin. "How about I go with you?"

"You would do that?"

"What are friends for?"

"But you said you have to go to the vet."

"Hm. Maybe we can go after I get back."

Tabbert's shoulders slumped. "Yeah, maybe."

"Or, maybe I can go with you while Clawedy-kins gets his boo-boo looked at." Gidget was coming out of the litter box by the back door. "I know more about the back yard than he does."

"Well... um... er..." Tabbert glanced nervously at me, then at Gidget, and then back at me. "You won't eat me, will you?"

"What kind of a cat do you think I am?" Gidget hissed.

"I didn't mean anything by that. It's just that..."

"I know, cats eat lizards. Do you know how many times I could have eaten you if I really wanted to?"

Tabbert's eyes were wide and glassy when he looked at Clawed. What Gidget said next settled it.

"And I'm probably the only one who can save you from being eaten by Tikky."

"Okay," Tabbert said. "Come out when Clawed leaves."

"Will do," Gidget said.

Feeling left out, Clawed growled.

"Sorry," Tabbert said. "I have to do this." He turned away, a heavy frown wrinkling his usually happy face.

After lunch, Sage none too gently put a very unwilling Clawed into the cat carrier. "See you later, Gidget. We'll be back before Ben gets home from work."

Clawed told Gidget. "And you be careful. Tabbert acts funny when he gets riled up."

Sage locked the door to the carrier. Clawed poked his nose out of the small wire-mesh window. He suddenly got all choked up and couldn't figure out why. "I mean it, Gidget. You be careful."

Gidget leaped up on the back of the couch and paced back and forth. "I'll be fine. Quit worrying."

Clawed could tell she was anxious to get going.

Sage picked up his carrier, closed the front door behind her, and turned the key in the lock.

Chapter 27

As soon as the car started

Gidget dashed out to the back patio, jumped through the hole in the screen, and slipped around to the gutter spout. She didn't see Tabbert, so she called him.

"Hey!" She still didn't see him. She called again. "Hey, chicken feet."

Tabbert peeked around the corner. He didn't know Gidget very well and wasn't used to being called names. He wished he hadn't agreed to go with her.

"Tabbert."

Tabbert's heart leaped. The Voice again. "Argh! I wish you'd stop doing that. You're going to give me a heart attack."

"Go with her."

"But…"

"Go."

Tabbert peered down at Gidget. She was sitting in a spot of sun with her eyes closed. He couldn't remember feeling this afraid in all his life, but it didn't seem like he had much of a choice. Either he stayed here and got harassed by that demanding voice, or he took his chances with a cattitude and a creepy gemstone.

Tabbert skittered to the ground. Staying a safe distance away, he called out to Gidget. "Yo."

She opened her eyes. It was impossible to get a catnap with the drone of heavy equipment operating next door. "It's about time. I don't have all day, you know."

"Okay then, let's go." Tabbert spun around, pausing only long enough to see that Gidget was following. He dashed through the rose harbor and ran along the cobbled path. There were no Blinglings napping in the shade.

Tabbert glanced over his shoulder. Gidget was right on his heels. He scooted into the tangle of brush that lined the edge of the clearing. He struggled to catch his breath. Gidget stopped next to him. Watching her out of the corner of his eye, he didn't move.

Not even winded, she turned to look at him. "What now?"

"I don't know."

They gazed out at the gem. Pulsing with a steady beat, the jewel radiated in the grass exactly where he'd left it the day before. There wasn't one Blingling anywhere, not on the flat rock where they'd been standing, not around the glittering showpiece that was larger than it had ever been – and to think, when he'd first found it in the treasure chest, it was small enough to fit in his hand.

Looking at the sticky scales on the bottoms of his front toes, he nodded.

"What?" Gidget asked.

"Do you see that thing?"

"Yes."

"Do you see anything else?"

"Like what?"

Tabbert frowned. "Like a couple of turtles, or Joey and Stevie—the mouse brothers."

Gidget peered through the brush and shook her head.

"Or a giraffe, or a pig?"

Gidget shook her head. "No, but I think you ought to know, I *have* seen them."

"You have?" Tabbert's mouth dropped wide open.

"I have."

"Then, why doesn't Clawed see them."

Gidget shrugged. "I don't know."

"Interesting."

"Do you see them now?" Gidget asked.

"No. I think that thing swallowed them. How can I help when I don't have the foggiest idea where they are?"

"What if you and I have a closer look." Gidget's fur prickled. An irritating rumble vibrated the ground.

Next door to Sage and Ben's house, a large truck was backing a trailer up to the excavator. One man was giving hand signals to another driving the machine. Would the grating noise of the construction ever stop?

Above the thrum of the motor, a resounding crack reached her ears, then another, and another. "Did you hear that?"

Already nervous, Tabbert spun in a circle. "I did."

The irritating ground vibrations stopped. The construction workers jumped out of the vehicles and stood in the cul-de-sac, waving their arms and talking excitedly.

"Hello there."

Gidget jumped. The fur along her neck and spine rose. She whirled to face the voice that had come from behind. "Tikky!"

That was all Tabbert needed to set his feet in motion. No big tom-cat was going to eat *him*. He dashed out of the bushes and ran across the clearing.

179

Gidget dashed after him. "Wait! Stop!"

Tikky called after them. "Hey. I just wanted to introduce myself."

Tabbert raced through the grass with Gidget in hot pursuit. He sped toward the menacing jewel that beamed with a throbbing blush.

When a loud cracking noise split the air, Tikky turned around and ran. He stopped and peered out of the wooded shadows. The ground in front of Gidget and Tabbert gave way and a monstrous hole opening in the earth swallowed the grass under their feet.

Tikky sprang from the bushes. He had to save Gidget.

Chapter 28

Gidget fumbled to grab hold of something

but the ground fell away beneath her. Her stomach tightened into a sickening knot as she plummeted through the air.

Unzipping its grassy covering to expose a growing cavity, a hungry maw opened in the earth and swallowed everything above it.

Slowly at first but with gathering speed, Gidget, and Tabbert, the jewel, the clearing, the excavator, and the half-completed paver driveway for the brand-new house screeched, squawked, ripped, and crashed into the ever-widening hole; the mailbox, a newly planted palm tree, and now the garage where Tikky had found the half-eaten sandwich was caving in too.

Paralyzed, Tikky wanted to turn and run, but couldn't. An earthquake? But no, not here, not Florida. Sinkhole! Clinging to the precarious edge of the roiling chasm, he peered into the hole but couldn't see a thing through the thick cloud of dust.

"Gidget!" He coughed and sneezed. "Gidget!" He could barely hear his own voice over the wrenching clang of metal against metal crashing onto construction debris and falling into the abyss.

The soggy ground where Gidget landed shuddered. She tried to climb out. Dirt crumbled around her. It rolled, tossed, and turned her, tail over whiskers. It filled her nose, her mouth, her ears. She couldn't breathe or open her eyes, and yet she fought, digging at the suffocating ball of earth that surrounded her.

Leaning into the gaping hole, Tikky called to her. "Gidget!"

Tabbert clung to the underside of the grass hanging over the edge. He pulled himself out of the hole, then ran up Tikky's leg, over his shoulder, across Tikky's cheek, down his back to the tip of his tail, and leaped onto the grass. He ran and kept on running across the yard, into the brush.

Stopping to catch his breath, Tabbert looked back over his shoulder, suddenly remembering Clawed's friend. "Gidget!"

He spun about, ran back across the yard, between Tikky's feet, and leapt into the sinkhole. Tikky grabbed for him as he went over the side.

Tabbert's tail broke loose. His feet paddled in mid-air. When he landed in the hole, he kept running. It was his fault Gidget was down there. "Gidget!"

Tikky meowed from up top. "Gidget!"

Tabbert scampered from fallen beam to metal fender. He searched under spinning tires. He clamored over clumps of grass, dirt, rocks, and sand that flowed in dry rivulets to the bottom like grains through the neck of an hour glass.

Ben was less than a tenth of mile from home when a police car, siren blaring, followed by a fire truck and an ambulance, forced him to pull off the road. After they passed, he pulled back onto the pavement and followed.

They pulled into his neighborhood. A policeman stopped him before he reached home. "Can't go in there, sir. Sinkhole opened right between the new house and this one."

Ben jumped out of the car. "That's my house!" He ran for his front yard.

"Sir, you can't park here." Ben kept going. "You can't go in there!" The officer grabbed Ben's arm.

"I have to. My wife…I've got pets in there."

The officer grabbed his arm. "It's not safe."

Sage came up behind them. "Oh, my gosh."

"Ma'am, you can't park there."

"Ben?"

He turned to her. "You okay?"

"Yes."

"I'm going in."

"But…"

"The cats."

"I've got Clawed," Sage said. "Look for Gidget. She usually hides in the bedroom closet."

Ben ran across the yard.

"Wait!" The officer ran after him.

"I'll move the cars," Sage said.

Neighbors were gathering in the cul-de-sac. Others came running down the street.

Sage threw Ben's keys to someone. "Can you move his car?" Without waiting for an answer, she ran to her own and jumped in behind the wheel.

"What's going on?" Clawed asked. "Why can't I get out?"

She parked three houses away, reached behind her seat, and patted Clawed's carrier. "I won't be long, Clawed. You're better off right here, for now." She got out and slammed the door.

Outside, a gusty wind whipped her long hair around her shoulders. Overcast skies threatened rain. Tropical storm warning; Clawed had heard it on the news that morning.

He meowed at the top of his lungs. "Where's Gidget? I want to come with you. Let me out."

Caterwauling did him no good. Resigned, he crouched in his carrier.

He worried while he waited. "I hope Gidget and Tabbert's okay. I hate being stuck in here." Pouting, Clawed crouched close to the wire-mesh door, ready to jump out first chance he got.

When the shifting and churning subsided, water gurgling from the same artesian source that fed Bling's butterfly pond slowly rose and filled the sinkhole. Gasoline from the construction equipment oozed in rainbows of greasy puddles over the top of the water.

Tabbert continued calling Gidget's name as he skittered over dirt and debris.

"Mmmffffffff."

Tabbert cocked an ear towards the sound. "Gidget?"

"I heard that. I'm coming down," Tikky yowled.

"No," Tabbert said. In the next instant, Tikky was standing over him.

Tabbert backed up a few steps. "Please don't eat me. I'm Gidget's friend. We have to get her out of here."

"I'm not going to eat you, reptile. Where is she?"

"Mmmffffffff."

Tikky and Tabbert stared at the spot the sound had come from. "Gidget!"

Calling her name, they ran back and forth, pawing at the dirt, and continued searching the sink hole even as the water level slowly rose higher as afternoon dimmed into evening.

Every time Tabbert called Gidget's name, her muffled answer sounded somewhere below his feet. Tikky dug. Tabbert called.

"Mmmffffffff." Each time, her cry became quieter.

Tikky meowed. "Gidget." He was soaked to the skin, his fur wet and matted, his voice cracked with fatigue…

All the while, the dry streamed in Bling crumbled into the growing sink hole.

Calling Gidget's name every few seconds, Ben scoured every room. He looked in the closets and under the beds with a flashlight. He even opened all the cabinet doors in case she'd gotten stuck in one.

Then he searched again…and again. He searched the back porch and looked in the litter box. Wind whipped at the loose screen. Seeing it gave him a twinge of hope. Maybe Gidget had gotten out through it.

Before he left the house, he grabbed a box of kitty crunchies.

He returned to Sage. "I didn't find her, but…" He told her about the hole in the screen. "I forgot to fix it. I'm glad now. Hopefully, she got out. It looks bigger than I remember. Maybe they've both been getting out."

She nodded. "That may explain the bruise on Clawed's head. It makes sense now."

Growing darkness swallowed the daylight. Neighbors shining lights into the hole, called out. "There's a cat down there!"

Ben and Sage ran to the edge of the hole. They both called out simultaneously. "Gidget!"

The neighbor's light shone on a big orange tomcat.

"That's Tikky."

Ben thrust his flashlight at Sage and dashed back to the house.

"Where are you going?"

"To get a ladder."

A policeman protested. "You can't go down there."

"Watch me," Ben stuffed the box of crunchies under his arm, took a hold of a ladder rails, and stepped onto a rung. "Sage, hand me the flashlight. Hopefully, Gidget's down there, too."

The policeman followed him down the ladder.

When they reached the bottom, Ben stepped off the ladder into ankle deep in water.

He shone the light around the chasm. The construction excavator lay on its side. One of its huge wheels spun slowly.

Clumps of grass, pavers from the new house's driveway, and tangled vegetation protruded out of dirt walls that loomed above his head.

Half crushed, the mailbox post had penetrated the excavator window and was stuck in the driver's seat. Its door hung open by one screw and swung slightly. Dark rivulets of sand streamed downward like the hole was alive.

Water bubbling up from the ground covered his feet within minutes. The sinkhole had tapped into the artesian spring.

Ben stared at the wreckage. "Whew, this is crazy down here. Smells like gas."

Sage's voice reached him from above. "Do you see Gidget? Hurry up and come out of there."

Ben's beam found Tikky. "Look at you, big fella. Is Gidget down here with you?" He and the policeman continued scanning the hole.

Tabbert scooted behind a large coquina rock when Ben pointed the light directly on him.

Tikky ran any time Ben got close. Talking softly, Ben stretched a treat-filled hand toward him. For once, food didn't entice him. He tried to climb out, but he couldn't get a grip on the sandy, crumbling walls. Gas fumes made his eyes water and set a sneezing fit on him so badly he had to stop to catch his breath. That's when Ben grabbed him.

Tikky wasn't about to let anybody shove him into a carrier, or confine him to a screened-in porch, or feed him treats like he was some pampered poodle. He yowled and scratched but could not get loose.

Ben clamped Tikky him under one arm and climbed the ladder out of the hole. When he set the frightened cat on the ground, Tikky fled.

Ben shook his head. No Gidget. What a catastrophe.

He and Sage spent a few minutes talking to the neighbors. The police weren't letting them back in the house, so they decided to spend the night in a hotel. When the firemen turned on their hoses and sprayed chemicals into the sinkhole to neutralize the gas, Ben and Sage said good-night to everyone.

Sage climbed in behind the steering wheel and fastened her seat belt. "How're you doing, Clawed?"

"Where's Gidget?" he asked.

Sage didn't answer. As she drove away, thunder boomed and lightning cracked like a shotgun blast. The black skies opened up and torrents of rain flooded the thirsty ground.

Chapter 29

It rained

non-stop for the next week, sometimes in sheets; other times, only a slight drizzle. The weather was as miserable as Clawed felt. While Sage and Ben went home every day to search for Gidget, he sat alone in the hotel room. He couldn't wait to get home and do some searching for himself.

Every day, he watched the progress on TV. Police officials, firemen, and engineers crawled in, out, around, and over the sinkhole. Cranes set up in the cul-de-sac removed and hauled away the ruined heavy equipment and most of the debris. Until engineers determined that the hole was not going to keep expanding and the surrounding properties were safe to live in again, they weren't going home.

News commentators reported that, even though the area wasn't normally susceptible to sink holes, the long drought and the heavy construction next door may have contributed to a once-in-a-life-time phenomenon that happened, because sometimes—things do.

Three weeks later, Clawed went home. It felt good to get back to the routine. Ah, there was nothing like his cat tower.

He searched the house. Gidget was still missing. He was about to sneak outside when Tabbert skittered up the gutter spout.

"It's about time you got back. I was starting to worry." He ran back and forth across the screen, then stopped. "Is Gidget around?"

"No. I thought you and she were going back to…Bling."

"Um…" Tabbert hesitated.

Clawed stared at him.

Tabbert gulped. "She was right behind me. And then the hole opened up."

"And?" Clawed was still staring.

"I didn't see her after that. We thought we heard her …

"We?"

"Me and Tikky. He was in there with me the whole time looking for her. But then the water got too high…" His voice trailed off.

Clawed turned and gazed at the rose arbor. "What about Bling? Is she out there?"

"Um…no."

"And the Blinglings?"

"You won't believe it."

"What?"

"Most of them are still there. The other day, I was looking for Gidget by the sinkhole. Strangest thing happened; A thin stream flowed away, in the opposition direction of the sinkhole. Next thing I know, it's breaking up into smaller drops and sliding *up* the bushes. I had to have a closer look. And what do you think I see?"

Clawed sighed. Tabbert, always with the drama. "What?"

"A whole bunch of Blinglings, and new ones too. Rabbits, penguins, reindeer."

"That's nice."

"You don't seem too excited about it."

"Sorry. I've never met a Blingling. The point IS, did you see Gidget?"

"No. And Lil's gone too."

Before long, Tikky was strutting around the yard again. It didn't bother Clawed like it used to. They had something in common. Gidget. Still, Clawed found it hard to admit he was jealous that Tikky had known Gidget longer than he had.

He missed her so bad, it hurt. When he could, Clawed jumped out the ripped screen and went to the woods to look for her. No one had found her in the sinkhole. Maybe she'd gotten out and run away.

Ben fixed the screen, and installed a cat door to the outdoors.

"Clawed…" He gave Clawed a stern look and waggled a finger in his face. "Try not to get hurt. There're coyotes out there. All kinds of dangerous things can take you away from us. Losing one cat is hard enough. We don't want to lose you, too."

Clawed meowed and rubbed his head on Ben's hand. The minute Ben went inside, Clawed was out the door. Nice!

That afternoon, Tabbert and Clawed searched every square inch of the grassy shore of the sinkhole-turned-pond. Neither had given up looking for Gidget.

Finding nothing, Clawed followed Tabbert through the rose arbor. A strange hum filled the air as they passed through it. Clawed shook his head. Weird. That had never happened to him before.

They got settled under the plumbago bush. Clawed was about to doze off when Tabbert jumped up.

"Hey, there's Necky, and Joey and Stevie."

Clawed opened one eye, then blinked…and blinked again.

Something plop-splashed into the butterfly pond. Moments later, a strange looking frog poked his nose out of the water.

"I can see them," Clawed said.

"See what?" Tabbert asked.

"Your friends, the Blinglings."

"Really?"

"Really."

"Gidget said she could see them too."

Clawed nodded. "I knew it."

With all those lives Gidget had talked about, and now, knowing that she'd been able to see the Blinglings, maybe—

"We've been thinking about this all wrong."

Tabbert's dewlap flared. "How so?"

"Maybe the reason we can't find Gidget is because she's... a Blingling now!" Clawed dashed out from under the bush.

Tabbert clung to one of Clawed's ears. "Where are you going?"

"To look for Gidget."

Chapter 30

Gidget turned her gaze…

to the clearing. Her clear faceted lines glinted in the afternoon sun. Piggy Pomp was busy polishing the lilies near the butterfly pond, a much bigger one than Gidget remembered. Since she'd become secretarycat of Bling, everything seemed bigger, colorful, and more vibrant.

The turtles chewed on greens growing through the cobbled walkway. Sage had probably planted the smorgasbord there for them.

No. Humans couldn't see the Blinglings. Could they?

Gidget had been able to, and she finally understood why. She'd been on her ninth life, and that was all cats got on the human plane of Earth. Stocker had told her that Bling was the next step to the clouds.

Towering over her, Stocker gazed out over the Town of Bling. "Before Lil took her new position, she told me you'd be a good steward of the garden. I agree." Stocker said. "She never remembered her past. Usually, when critters pass from one life to the next, they don't. That may have been a mistake.

"I'm letting you keep your memories, Gidget. The pain of them will dim with time, but hopefully, having them will help you keep the Blinglings in line."

Gidget looked across the clearing. The Blinglings, lovely with their iridescent facets, were busy with their work; and, there, shading themselves from the afternoon sun, were Clawed and Tabbert.

"When are you going to show yourself to Tabbert?"

"Already have," Gidget answered.

"And, Clawed?"

"I don't know. I miss him. Do you think he'll recognize me?"

198

"He sees the Blinglings now. With a bit more faith, he'll recognize you."

"But, do I look like Lil?" Still not used to being able to see through herself, Gidget stared at her faceted paw.

Stocker bowed his head. He touched her nose with his. "You look like Gidget."

He turned away, then glanced back at her over his shoulder. "Remember this, Gidget. It's more important to take care of what we have than it is to own a shiny new bauble.

"Tell the Blinglings to cultivate flowers of forgiveness, friendship, and love. Those are the real treasures that help a garden grow."

Then, as usual, he disappeared.

Chapter 31

After a time

the underground artesian spring filled the sinkhole to its brim. The neighbors worked together to create a park around it and around the new house which was finally completed.

Clawed slipped outside and passed through the rose arbor into Bling. The sun sparkled on Blinglings working at their assigned tasks. Thinking about taking a nap, he sat by the butterfly pond.

Magical forces that he could barely understand had taken Gidget. *Jeopardy* trivia didn't even come close to intriguing him as much as the goings on of Bling did. He was determined to learn as much as he could about the town. But first, he'd go look for Gidget one more time. Maybe if he asked the Dilitz maids….

He remembered what Tabbert had said. "'Touch the surface of the water. The ripple is like a radio signal. It will call them.'"

Wishing for the thousandth time that he could see Gidget, he looked at his paw, then gingerly tapped the water. A sudden burst of sunlight blinded him…and in a cat's breath, he had a bubble-thing on his head and was being dragged through the water so fast it made him dizzy.

When he came to a stop, two Dilitz maids were floating by his side in the motionless blueness. A treasure chest hovered in front of him. Radiant colors drew him closer. He backed away. He wasn't going anywhere near that thing. That's what had gotten Tabbert in trouble and those Blinglings too.

Hoping he wouldn't be stuck in the watery cavern for too long, Clawed settled into his nap.

"Row, row, row your boat, gently down the stream, merrily, merrily, merrily, merrily…"

THE END

Read on for Chapter 1 of ***Dog Days,*** Book 2 of the *"I, Clawed"* adventures.

Chapter 1

After everything that had happened,

Clawed couldn't help wondering. What was going mess with his day?

He had come to expect—something would.

For some reason, he was sleeping a lot lately. He didn't feel like his usual, bright-eyed and bushy-tailed self. Maybe because of the oppressive heat.

Or maybe because he'd been having the strangest dream about Gidget who used to live with Sage, and Ben, and him, key words being, "used to." Gidget and Clawed had been through a lot together, but he hadn't seen her since she'd become Secretarycat of Bling, even though he'd searched everywhere inside and out until he thought his eyes would bug out of his head.

His heart wrenched in his chest. He missed her.

Tabbert had seen her. Clawed felt a bit resentful about that. Still, how did one go about seeing a magical creature small as his own paw and see-through-ish?

Nothing stirred in the cool air-conditioned house. Too quiet. It was humid and hot as a baked potato, but being outside always helped Clawed feel better.

Not meaning to be unkind about his best friend Tabbert, a Florida anole, ~~~ Clawed half hoped he wasn't around. His nonstop babble could be annoying at times, and Clawed wasn't in the mood for chitchat.

He yawned. Sage and Ben must have gone to the Humane Society thrift store, or—somewhere. Clawed jumped off the back of the couch and went to the kitchen to check out his dish.

After gobbling up a smidgeon of crunchies, he slipped through the partially open sliding glass door out to the screened-in pool patio. He nosed around a bit, passed by his carpeted cat tower, then jumped through the cat door to go outside.

His eyes steamed over. Yuk. August. Dog days. He considered going back in, but the quiet lull of the day drew him out.

As quietly as he could and keeping his claws crossed, Clawed kept to the shadows close to the house. He didn't see Tabbert anywhere. He tiptoed around to the side yard, slunk across the well-groomed grass, hurried past the sinkhole-pond where Gidget had disappeared, and headed for the woods. Maybe it would be a bit cooler there.

He entered a clearing in the middle of a dense forest of pines, palms, and oaks, where kids sometimes camped overnight or hung out for a day. It looked the same as always. Big logs for sitting on surrounded a fire pit ringed with smooth river rocks.

Hoping for a chicken-wing bone or a piece of scorched hot dog, Clawed sniffed the cold ashes. Nothing. Not that he was hungry. He was well-fed. His round belly was a testament to that.

He sat back and gazed around. His studious inspection stopped on the rusted shopping cart that usually stood, full of wood, near the fire pit.

The cart had been turned onto its side. A piece of plywood with a hole in it about as big around as his middle was zip-tied to the top. A cover? For what?

It didn't seem like anyone had visited the clearing for a while.

Ahh. Peace and quiet.

Not.

"Hello there."

Clawed resisted the urge to shake his head. "Hey, Tikky. What're you doing?"

"Not much. Too hot."

"I hear that."

Maybe if Clawed kept going, Tikky would get the hint that he didn't feel like company right now. Fat chance. Tikky didn't seem to care what others thought.

Not that that's always a bad thing. When critters get caught up worrying about what others think, their brains can turn to scrambled eggs.

Sheesh. Clawed was starting to think like Tabbert. Hopefully he didn't start babbling like he did. Clawed slipped through the brush and headed toward the citrus grove.

Tikky stayed right on his tail. "What's new at your house?" Obviously, he was in the mood for company.

The buzz of the summer cicadas drilled through Clawed's head. He sat, licked his paw, then washed his face. A dragonfly whizzed by. Tikky sat, too.

"Not much," Clawed said.

They sat in the shade of an orange tree.

They'd gone whisker to whisker a few times, but once they'd gotten to know each other, they managed to get along.

Tikky lived in the woods by his own choice. It must have been tough finding food out there sometimes. But by the looks of his round belly, he found enough to eat. It helped that Sage put treats out for him every day.

His fluffy, long fur looked matted and dirty, but he didn't seem to mind.

It was Clawed's opinion that appearances were important. He wiped his whiskers after every meal and washed every day to keep his black coat looking shiny and sleek. Folks called him a Halloween cat.

He was about to doze off when something thudded against his side. It felt like he'd been hit by a huge spit ball.

"Oof." Tabbert bounced off him and fell over backwards. Just as quickly, he was up on his feet again. Eyeing Tikky, he scooted closer to Clawed and clung to his fur. Tabbert would probably never trust that Tikky wouldn't eat him.

Since he'd became friends with Tabbert, Clawed had stopped catching lizards. Since Tabbert could change colors, from green to yellow or gray, even brown, Clawed didn't want to make a mistake and eat someone in his family.

"What's your hurry, reptile?" Tikky asked.

Tabbert straightened his shoulders. His dewlap flared. "How many times do I have to ask you not to call me that? I have a name."

"Whatever." Tikky yawned and looked away.

"You'd better skedaddle," Tabbert said. "There's a big dog chasing me."

The words were no sooner out of his mouth when a sorry-looking, sort-of-yellow dog crashed into the clearing. Clawed made a beeline for the closest tree. He scrambled up the trunk and crouched in the crook of the lowest branch. Tabbert clung to his ear.

Tikky darted in another direction, squeezed through the hole in the board covering the shopping cart, and huddled in the corner.

Yellow dog sniffed the air, then sniffed the ground and followed a scent to the base of the tree where Clawed and Tabbert sat above his reach.

A bark exploded from his mouth. He lunged at the tree trunk. Thank goodness he couldn't climb. But he sure tried.

After a while, he quit barking. His continued sniffing took him to the shopping cart. Tikky crouched within its steel confines. Barking like a maniac, the dog ran circles around it.

Tikky hissed and growled. Every time the dog got too close, Tikky swiped his claws through the metal mesh, connecting with the dog's nose a few times.

That dog's bark became more aggressive. Tikky could hold his own, unless the dog got the lid off that cart, which was what he tried to do next. He chomped on an edge of the board, scratched at it, barked at it, and tore at it.

Whoever had attached that board had done a crazy good job. It held even when the dog grabbed one of the wheels and dragged the cart around the clearing. Tikky yowled and held on. Every time that dog got his face too close, Tikky tore him up.

Clawed stayed glued to the tree limb with Tabbert hanging over the tip of his nose.

And then, Tabbert fell. Grabbing nothing, his feet swam in the air. He landed on the dog's nose, leaped, and hit the ground running. The dog took off after him.

Annoying babbler or not, Clawed had to help Tabbert. He jumped down from the tree and dashed after the barking canine that was now trying to climb another tree.

Clawed leaped and landed on the dog's back and dug in. To his surprise, Tikky had followed and was clinging to the hound's neck.

The dog howled and rolled over and over on the ground. Clinging to a hulk of raging mutt wasn't a fun battle. Clawed about lost his breath every time he rolled over onto his back.

Eventually, he shook the cats off, turned tail, and fled. Clawed would have chased him, but wanted to make sure Tabbert was okay.

Clawed yelled into the tree. "Tabbert, you up there?"

"Who are you looking for? Your little lizard friend? Tasty little fellow." Tikky licked his chops and grinned.

Maybe Clawed was agitated from all the excitement, or maybe he was tired of Tikky's pomp and fluff. He turned and swiped the grin off Tikky's face and followed that up with a cuff to his right ear.

He fell backwards but immediately leaped to his feet. "Hey. I was kidding."

Clawed glared at him with bared teeth. "Not funny."

For once, Tikky had the good sense not to grin again. There was a time when they'd have been at each other's throats, but a few months ago they'd worked together to save Gidget.

She was special. Because of her, somehow Clawed and Tikky had sorted out their differences.

Clawed wasn't sure why Tikky brought out the worst in him. Perhaps he should apologize even though he didn't want to. "Sorry I hit you."

Tikky shrugged. "Didn't feel a thing. You really ought to work out more." He sniffed and pointed. "Over there on that log."

Clawed looked to where he was pointing and spied Tabbert.

Clawed ran to him. "You okay?"

"Couldn't be better." He made a motion to swish his tail, only it wasn't there.

"Missing something?" Tikky asked.

Tabbert looked over his shoulder and down his back. "Oops, that mutt must have been closer than I thought. Oh well, it'll grow back. I think I'll head home. All that excitement made me kind of sleepy."

"Come on," Clawed said. "I'll take you. I've had enough excitement for one day, too."

Tabbert skittered up Clawed's leg and clung to his shoulder. "See you around, Tikky."

"Later. Hey, by the way," Tikky said. "I recognize that mutt. That's Leroy. He used to live in a trailer at the edge of the woods, that is, before it burnt down. People up and left him. We met once. Came to a men-in-the-woods kind of respect. He goes his way. I go mine. You know what I mean?"

"Yeah, sure." If he were being honest, Clawed didn't really understand. He lived in a clean, comfortable house with people who fed him every day, petted him, and even watched TV with him.

"Anyway," Tikky went on. "I'm going to sneak over to Hudson's farm, see if I can't catch a meal with the barn cats. Maybe stay and play for a bit. Later." He headed into the orange grove.

"Hey, Tikky," Tabbert said.

Tikky stopped and turned around. "Yeah?"

"Thanks." Tabbert looked from Tikky to Clawed. "Both of you, for…you know, keeping that mongrel from getting me."

"No problem, reptile," Tikky said. "If anybody's going to eat you, I guarantee you, it's not going to be some mangy old hound."

He winked and turned away.

Tabbert's eyes squinted into tiny slits.

Clawed shook his head.

As they headed back to the house, Clawed and Tabbert talked about the dog.

"He looks dirty and pretty skinny. It's hard to believe that people would actually abandon their pet. Did you see those teeth? It doesn't look like he's ever brushed them. His breath is really bad, like he's been eating rotten eggs or something." Tabbert shivered. "I could smell him breathing down my neck when he was chasing me."

"You're lucky he didn't eat you."

"What if he's out there the next time we go back out?"

Clawed didn't want to think about that.

They didn't talk again the rest of the way home.

When the gutter downspout where Tabbert lived came into view, he climbed down Clawed's tail and ran across the yard as fast as his little legs could carry him. He'd had a bad fright today. No need to say good bye. They'd catch up later.

Clawed nosed through the cat door to the pool patio, padded past his cat tower, then through the smaller cat door into the air conditioned quiet of the house. Ahh, a nap on the back of the couch seemed like a good idea.

He was about to jump up when a strange sight froze him.

The fur down his back stood straight up. His throat constricted as he struggled to keep from growling. He ducked under the couch to investigate from there.

On the floor in front of the coffee table, a lump of black fur lay on a checkered pillow. Clawed sniffed double time, his nostrils flapping like mosquito wings. Yuk. Antiseptic. A blue and white bandage was wrapped around one back leg, and half the fur up the other back leg had been shaved off. Stitches crisscrossed its body in several places—across its belly, along one ear, under one eye, down the other leg.

What was a puppy—a mangled one at that, doing at Clawed's house? He aimed to find out.

It was easier to deal with a puppy in the house than to think about the mean dog in the woods.

Would it ever be safe to go out there again?

213

www.ingramcontent.com/pod-product-compliance
Lightning Source LLC
Chambersburg PA
CBHW031330170626
46807CB00002B/629